MW00834019

"We took our

"Exactly.
And it was a second too long wasn't it?"

"My God, Sage, it was just a simple kiss." Hawke instantly regretted the callousness of that comment when he noticed the rage creep into her eyes, then immediately evaporate into genuine pain.

"It was not just a kiss, Hawke." She turned to face him, "It was my first kiss. My first kiss since Eric. And it was not simple. To me. A kiss is not simple if it made me feel so warm that when it was over I was surprised that it was still snowing. My mind celebrated the sensations of that kiss with such an explosion of colors the dusk momentarily blinded me." She buried her face in her palms, pressed her fingertips in her eyes, and sighed heavily. "I think that my antipathy could be directly related to the fact that those few stolen moments have altered my life forever. And to you it was just a simple kiss."

Hawke only heard her confession hidden between the lines and his heart whispered. *Oh my God, she loves me.* He wanted to celebrate, to embrace her and swing her in a circle and kiss her fully, deeply and then carry her away to the…what was he thinking? Down boy, down.

"I believe in signs, Hawke. Even someone insensitive to signs should surely see through this one. While I as so preoccupied with 'just a kiss' as you so delicately put it, my daughter, my most precious Pia, disappeared. That is clearly a message. Loud and clear. That kiss was a mistake. A huge, unforgivable mistake." Her chin quivered and tears trailed down her perfect complexion. "My God! What have I done?"

Thistle Dew

by

ALee Drake

This is a work of fiction. Names, characters, places, and incidents either are the product of the author's imagination or are used fictitiously, and any resemblance to actual persons living or dead, business establishments, events, or locales, is entirely coincidental.

Thistle Dew

COPYRIGHT ©2009 by Andrea L. Kaczor

All rights reserved. No part of this book may be used or reproduced in any manner whatsoever without written permission of the author or The Wild Rose Press except in the case of brief quotations embodied in critical articles or reviews.
Contact Information: info@thewildrosepress.com

Cover Art by *Nicola Martinez*

The Wild Rose Press
PO Box 708
Adams Basin, NY 14410-0706
Visit us at www.thewildrosepress.com

Publishing History
First Faery Rose Edition, 2009
Print ISBN 1-60154-643-2

Published in the United States of America

Dedication

To Wladziu, my happily ever after,
To my children Kirsten, Mark, Sarah,
Stephen, Aleta, Robert, and Adam,
To Mom and Dad,
Heartfelt thanks to Sarah
for your brilliant suggestions.
To the Diamonds, Bill and Janine,
To Dee who said this was the one,
And to Jamie West, my editor,
for her expertise and intuition.

Chapter 1

He was late. The other writers had probably already arrived at the retreat. Hawke loved his new ride. The bike was comfortable and he stretched his legs to rest new boots on shiny metal stirrups.

Earlier this afternoon, the air teased with an Indian summer warmth, so much so that he considered leaving his new leather jacket home. Even after he left the little roadside diner a few hours later, the evening sun still radiated some heat as the purple sky blazed with iridescent orange and gold streaks.

He was intrigued by the intensity of his senses, the heightened awareness of his surroundings as he zipped over narrow byways and two lane highways that meandered through forests, farmlands and small one traffic light towns. The fresh scent of pine, the woodsy odor of moist leaves and moss drifted in the air. His stomach rumbled when he caught the dinnertime smells of a barbeque.

Now it was almost midnight. Despite his armor of leather, the chill cut through him like ice shards. He loved the feel of raw power, loved the roar like a primal animal as he accelerated and especially loved the freedom, like flying through the night, leaning into the turns and hugging the saddle with his thighs.

The only thing missing, the only item absent from his virgin motorcycle experience was a woman. He envisioned her long legs straddling him from behind, her arms wrapped around him, her head resting on his shoulder and her warmth caressing his back. It seemed the only accessory he couldn't purchase at the dealership was the one he wished for most.

He slowed down as he approached the limits of the small Adirondack village of Silver Creek. A block or two of street lights, a traffic light at the intersection and the interior glow of a doughnuts shop greeted him. At the drive through window a uniformed officer leaned on the fender of his black and white and nodded to an old man walking his dog.

As much as he craved a hot cup of coffee, his GPS informed him that the Thistle Dew Bed and Breakfast was located just two miles outside of town. He would ask for something hot when he got there.

The single beam of the bike guided along the back country road, startled a deer who darted back into the woods, and highlighted a small sign and arrow the directed him to turn up a long dirt driveway.

Hawke paused and stared up at the dwelling as he pulled off his gloves. It was a simple white clapboard house with windows guarded by black shutters. A wrap-around porch was illuminated by a single lantern highlighting pots of gold and orange mums and vacant wicker chairs. A slight breeze caused one rocker to move eerily back and forth.

It was the single glow from inside that beckoned him with a silent 'Welcome Home'.

He filled his lungs with the crisp country air, tugged at a pinch caused by his new black chaps and started toward the house. The pounding of his biker's boots on the brick kept rhythm with the pounding in his chest.

The motorcycle, his latest toy, should have been put away until spring, but the urge tugged at him with relentless strength and he'd succumbed. Now he just felt frozen to the bone.

The oak and stained glass door opened. "Welcome Mr..."

"Hawke." He entered the warmth, set his backpack on the floor as she closed the door and slid the bolt. "Just Hawke. I apologize for being so late, Miss..."

"Mrs. Winters."

He had erroneously pictured the owner of the bed and breakfast as an older lady, the grandmotherly type. He would gladly have skipped the meat loaf special at Walt's Diner and the subsequent conversation with a lonely waitress if he had known. If he had known this lovely woman was here, worked here, was waiting for him here, he would have skipped dinner altogether.

He inhaled slowly, deeply offering a silent word of thanks.

The woman standing before him now was a vision, like dessert for the eyes. So visually delicious he could almost taste her. Sweet, smooth and classy like an expensive after dinner liqueur - maybe a crème de menthe. He touched his lips with his tongue, desperate for a sample.

This is the woman, he thought. The one I've imagined pressed up against me on my motorcycle tonight. The one I've imagined forever, curled up like a kitten beside me on the sofa as we read, smiling as we sit across from each other during a candle lit dinner, stretched beneath me offering each other dessert. This is the woman.

He smiled as he watched her chew nervously on her bottom lip and curl an itinerant lock of hair behind one ear. He struggled not to touch to confirm that she was real.

"That's fine. I had a few things left to do for tomorrow's meal." She led him into the great room where heat radiated from the fireplace.

He followed, appreciating the way the tip of her

single braid gently brushed the small of her back as she walked.

He forced himself to look away long enough to appreciate the room. Sturdy old hand hewn beams held up the ceiling, weathered barn wood paneled the walls and pasture stones made the fireplace. A plump leather couch, loveseat and lounge chairs held chintz and paisley throw pillows and small round breakfast tables each with two or four branch chairs made up the dining area. The room smelled of wood smoke and evergreen. He looked forward to the weekend.

"Very nice." He nodded and smiled to reiterate his compliment.

****

Sage returned the friendly smile.

"Thank you." And when she saw a gleam in his eyes that was clearly not meant for the antique oak high board she added, "My husband and I were very pleased with the final outcome of this room."

This room that suddenly felt much too warm.

"You must be freezing." She gestured for him to sit in a chair by the hearth.

He unzipped his leather jacket. "Actually the leather does a great job of keeping the wind from going through."

He draped it over the arm of the chair and Sage noticed how his black turtleneck sweater clung tightly to his broad chest.

He needs a haircut, she thought, as he attempted to comb back his thick dark hair with both hands, then shook his head like a wet puppy. That impromptu gesture caused Sage's heart to skip a beat.

He turned toward the huge stone fireplace where bright orange embers still promised heat. Crossing the room with a long, confident stride, he knelt down, exposing his open palms to the warmth.

Sage could not control her gaze as she blatantly appreciated the black leather chaps that protected his legs from the cold, and quite nicely defined his tight denim-clad derriere. "Then those parts of you that are not covered in leather must be frozen stiff."

OH MY GOD!!!! Had she really spoken out loud????

Thankfully, he didn't respond so she tried to recover some dignity. "I was thinking that your hands must be really cold."

He chuckled, a deep pleasant sound that ignited a spark that made a blush color her face. "I have leather gloves too, but yes, the heat in this room is very comforting."

Just then an itinerant gust came down the chimney and sent on orange spray out onto the hearth. Hawke jumped back and wiped at one glowing ember that embedded in his sleeve.

"Oh, I'm sorry." Sage took his hand to see that he hadn't been burned, but dropped it quickly as his touch scorched her fingers.

She wiped her hands on the flowered terrycloth dishtowel she wore tucked in the waistband of her jeans, then smoothed back a lock of hair that had too frequently tickled her nose. "May I get you a cup of coffee?"

"Thanks."

She retreated to the kitchen and was startled to see that he followed closely behind. "Are you hungry?" Sage turned to the oven. "I have some apple pie left from dinner."

"With ice cream?"

When he smiled his blue eyes crinkled and twinkled with something akin to mischief as he sat on a tall stool at the counter.

Unsettled by the immediate attraction, she gave him an uneasy glance. "I'll bring it out to you, Mr. Hawke. Guests take their meals in the great room."

Sage poured coffee into a mug, and set the carton of ice cream on the counter. He ignored the sugar and sipped the black brew.

"It's Hawke. Just Hawke." He rested his elbows on the counter top. "And I actually prefer to eat in the kitchen...if it's all right. I assume the others have gone to bed. I'd really appreciate your company while I thaw out." He cupped his hands around the warm mug. "The temperature must have dropped twenty degrees in the last hour."

She placed a scoop of ice cream onto his slice of pie, "I think it would be best if you..."

He smiled. "Please."

Dimples. Oh God. And such charm. Sage knew she should say no but already, her hostess-mode kicked in and took over. She nodded, then set the dessert before him and wiped her hands on the dishtowel. "Isn't it a little late in the season to be riding a bike?"

"This is our first trip together." He paused to eat a bite.

She noticed lovely lips as his tongue licked away a bit of cinnamon and apple. Sage shook herself mentally, why was she noticing these things?

"The sun was glorious this afternoon. I couldn't resist."

She smiled, silently remembering when Eric had taken her out on their inaugural ride on his new motorcycle as newlyweds. She loved snuggling up to Eric's back, head resting on his shoulder, arms wrapped in a loving hug. She teased him by letting her hands slip below his belt, felt him catch his breath and she would giggle.

"Mrs. Winters..." He cleared his throat. Hawke had moved to the small display shelf hanging by the back door. He lifted a golf ball decorated with a blue flower with a yellow center. He set the decorated golf ball back in its place. Beside it hung a broken putter,

6

its head resting on red felt, the shaft protected by sweat stained leather wrapping hung down beside the door frame. "I'd like to offer my sincere, although belated, condolences on the death of your husband."

"Thank you," she whispered, suddenly unsettled. How did he know? He was from another state. Was it Maine?

"I read it in your local paper. Archives. Research."

She hated that news story and photograph. Especially the photograph. It was an impersonal story about the freak accident that killed the young bed and breakfast owner. Speeders on the highway, trying to outrun the police, careened onto the shoulder, hit a ditch and went soaring onto the eleventh green of the Castlewood Golf Course, killing Eric instantly.

Sage tried to still the trembling in her hands. She watched the second hand tick ever so slowly so he could not read the fear in her eyes.

"Usually, before I travel, I like to familiarize myself with the social climate of my destination." Hawke took a forkful of warm pie, then closed his eyes. "Delicious."

She suddenly felt extremely vulnerable, unsafe. "Excuse me a moment."

She hurried through the connecting door that let to her private living room. This stranger knew about her. Knew that her husband died, knew that she had lost her champion. She leaned on the closed door, breathing deeply to calm her panic attack. What was she doing anyway? How could she continue the dream without him? The bed and breakfast dream was not hers alone. It was a dream she and Eric had shared. He had been her guardian. Now she was allowing strangers to reside in her home. People she knew nothing about. Men she knew nothing about. And this man looked exceedingly dangerous in black leather chaps. Her stomach twinged with fear. Or was it something else altogether? After several deep breaths to gather her composure, she returned to the kitchen.

****

Eric loved it when there was a breeze on the porch. He could swing in the hammock or rock in one of the old rockers without notice.

He felt the uneasy tension enter the room with the stranger and recognized its reality. He could see the bluish current of attraction arced between Sage and the man like downed wires in a storm. He blew a sigh into the fire, pleased that an ember made the stranger jump back.

Eric watched the scene unfold in the kitchen. Watched the appreciative yet shy gleam in the stranger's eyes as Sage bent to get the pie from the oven showing off her cute little heart-shaped bottom. Eric watched as the man focused on the butterfly tattoo that peeked from her lower spine when she reached into the freezer to put the carton away.

Eric watched as Sage unconsciously licked her lips when a drop of ice cream lingered on the strangers lip.

He watched.

And he knew.

This would be the man.

The man who would love his girls as Eric himself did.

Chapter 2

When her guests were finally all tucked into their rooms for the night, Sage breathed a sigh of relief and finished up in the kitchen. She looked out the window to the barns. Most of the alpacas were settled for the night, but as always the alpha male, Chakra, stood patiently at the fence, waiting for her to lock the door and switch off the light before he found a place to rest.

"G'night Chakra." She whispered. She put the fireplace screen in place, turned on a dim light in the corner of the room, then softly padded to the rooms behind the kitchen; her sanctuary. In the small pink bedroom, Sage tiptoed to check on her daughter Pia, who slept soundly as she snuggled with her stuffed animals. Sage gently pulled the blanket over Pia, kissed her cheek and finally, convinced that all was well, collapsed exhausted into her own bed.

And once again the lonely, mournful feeling crept into the bed beside her, wrapped its icy cold arms around her and squeezed until tears slid down her face and wet her pillow. Sleep eluded her while busy incomprehensible visions of motorcycles, golf carts and cowboys raced through her mind. She greeted the sunrise as exhausted as she had been the night before.

Mornings always came too soon. She climbed out of bed, tiptoed in to check on Pia, then headed for a rousing shower. A quick blow dry and a braid, a smudge of concealer to hide the tell tale dark circles beneath her eyes. She dressed simply in slacks and royal blue sweater, checked sleeping Pia once more and proceeded to the kitchen. She stopped at the back door to wave to Chakra who leaned over the fence as he did every morning to wait for her greeting. Apparently satisfied, Chakra, nodded his furry head and strode off to the far end of the pasture.

Sage loved her kitchen. When Eric was alive he teasingly complained that they spent more time in the kitchen than in the bedroom. Sage loved to cook. She loved trying new recipes and he loved being the taste tester. Sage watched the birds flutter around the nearly empty feeder while lost in year old memories.

The guests were already pouring mugs of coffee from the urn when Sage brought out the first platter of French toast. They were a hungry bunch, enjoying baked apples, and fresh fruits, as well as bacon and sausages. They all seemed to be talking animatedly about their most recent publications, Pulitzers or projects. It was an overwhelming group.

This was Eric's dream. A voracious reader, he'd envisioned having writer's retreats at Thistle Dew to meet his favorite authors, and give them a place to work with other writers without day to day distraction. It was the least he could do to coax them to create the wondrous entertainment from the books he loved. And now it was Sage's livelihood. Sage was pleased to see Eric's dream through. She felt anxious at first, intimidated at the thought of having well known authors here, in her small country Inn. But after meeting them, watching them, listening to them, she discovered she really liked these fascinating people. She now had a booklist to read throughout the year. And the reality of annual author retreats made Sage feel connected to Eric through his dream.

Sage watched and listened as she moved from kitchen to dining room, ever ready with the coffee pot and whisking empty plates off the tables.

All heads turned as Maribelle, a popular sci-fi erotica author, came downstairs fashionably late.

"Good morning all." Maribelle greeted, although her gaze clearly remained focused on Hawke as he sat talking with the others. "My, just look at the pretty butterfly. Six months hiatus in your cocoon has done you well." She placed a well-manicured hand on his shoulder, "Who would've thought."

Sage wondered what Maribelle meant. She knew Hawke's motorcycle was new. Maybe Maribelle meant his black leather jacket and too-tight jeans that looked very sexy. Maybe the bike brought out a side of Hawke Maribelle had never seen. What had he been like before?

"Thank you, Maribelle. Somewhere in there I'm sure I heard a compliment." Hawke stood, offering her his seat. "Now, if you'll excuse me, I have to go over my notes for tomorrow."

"In your room?" Maribelle smiled. "Would you like company?"

"As tempting as that offer sounds," He stood and held the chair signaling for her to be seated, "No."

At the same table, Sage topped off best-selling author Dakota Hayes' coffee and silently applauded Hawke's polite refusal. Looking at Dakota, she marveled that someone so famous was lodging at her little Thistle Dew Inn. Eric's dream, indeed.

Maribelle took the seat Hawke vacated completely unaffected by Hawke's dismissal.

For most of the morning Sage's guests were quiet, although periodically someone would slip on a jacket and take a walk outside through the gardens or to pet the soft fur of the friendly alpacas.

Sage was preparing her meals for Sunday. The number of guests would triple as the professionals offered workshops and mentoring clinics to aspiring writers. If the weather cooperated, the groups would meet in various settings around the property: the gazebo in the Golden garden, where the chrysanthemums, rudbeckia, and marigolds were at their glorious best, or the patio where weathered wicker furniture and potted plants offered a forest cottage atmosphere.

An arrangement of Adirondack chairs sat beneath a trio of white birch and another grouping of lawn chairs waited a distance away beneath a tall Japanese Maple tree proudly displaying its Merlot-colored leaves.

Inside, safely away from the autumn nip in the air, a crackling fire in the great room could spark lively conversations among a small assembly and another gathering could meet in the more formal surroundings of the living room.

Sage had worked to make Thistle Dew as inviting and homey as possible. Eric had taken care of the outside, she'd taken care of the inside. That was their deal. Sage took a moment to look out the kitchen window at the alpacas, contentedly munching grass. "Eric, do you even know how successful Thistle Dew is?" She whispered.

Sage heard a rhythmic tinkling and had to lean closer to the window to see the metal striker swing in the breeze like a pendulum, and ping against the triangle. The melodious vibrations made Sage envision an angel playing his instrument while relaxing on a cloud.

Pia came into the kitchen rubbing the sleep from her eyes. "I heard Daddy calling us to eat." She padded across the hardwood floors and reached up to Sage. Sage lifted Pia onto her hip. "You're getting heavy, Sweet Pea."

"Let me see Daddy ringing the funny bell." Pia leaned over to see the triangle's striker still swaying.

"Did you talk to my daddy this morning?" Pia placed both her palms on Sage's face, stared into her mother's eyes and waited for a no-nonsense reply.

Sage felt a chuckle start, but regarding the serious tone of her daughter she only nodded.

"Well, he's answering you." Her childish tone implied impatience. If Pia had been a teenager she might have added 'duh.'

Sage carried Pia over to sit at the counter. "What kind of answer?" She set a spoon and bowl on the counter. "Huh, smartie pants?"

"Well," Pia squeezed her eyes shut as if seriously contemplating an answer. "It is a happy sound, so... it means YES." Pia nodded with surety. "What did you ask him Mommy?"

Sage felt a chill crawl up her backbone. The same as the chill she felt when Eric would draw on her back with his finger and recite the rhyme: 'X marks the spot, with a dash and a dot, the upsies and downsies, a big question mark. Along came a warm summer breeze...' then he would gently puff down the collar of her shirt and she would get goosebumps and giggle. That same chill.

"I asked him if he is watching over his little Pia."

Pia's little face glowed. "He is."

"Yes, Sweet Pea, he is." Sage gave her a hug and some breakfast then continued other preparations in thoughtful silence.

Pia placed the empty bowl on the counter beside the sink. "That's all, Momma." She climbed on the counter stool. "Now what can I do?"

"Would you like to fold the napkins?" Sage pulled the napkins from the dryer and piled them on the counter. Four year old Pia, eagerly tended to the task, seriously meeting corner to corner, neatly folding to make sure the embroidered wildflower pattern was centered perfectly.

"How's that?" Pia held up her first attempt.

"Perfect." Sage complimented and Pia beamed.

In her peripheral vision Sage caught movement outside in the yard. The tall man pulled the collar of his leather jacket up to ward off the autumn chill. She watched, intrigued, as Hawke crossed the lawn to the split rail fence that separated the yard from the alpaca playground. He looked so appealing, easy on the eyes Grandma would say, as he casually leaned against the fence, elbows resting on the top rail. He seemed to be talking. To himself? Maybe plotting. Sage had read somewhere that authors often talked to themselves when they were working through a scene.

But then she watched as Chakra inched his way toward the fence. He'd take a step forward then dance a sidestep, then move forward again. Chakra, the beast who only allowed Eric to scratch the length of his nose without so much as a nip, was actually letting Hawke stroke the fine fur of his neck. Maybe Chakra has finished grieving for Eric. I wonder if I'll ever stop missing him so much. She shook her head. No, probably not.

Just then Hawke threw back his head and laughed, and Sage wished for a brief second that she stood beside Hawke, sharing a light moment with him, feeling his warmth as she snuggled next to him.

Without warning, he turned and waved to her. She leaned back, pretending she hadn't been caught watching him. Admiring him. Daydreaming about him.

At noon Sage rang the triangle Eric made to call the wanderers in for lunch. She recalled Eric as he proudly hung the newly forged triangle on the porch and in the jangle she heard echoes of their laughter as X-rays later showed that his swollen throbbing thumb had been broken in the process.

The writers entered the house still actively conversing. Each hung jackets on the pegs in the entry.

"I'm famished." Norman heaped his bowl of chili with a generous sprinkling of freshly grated cheeses. He stood mesmerized for a long moment. Sage watched him smile wistfully. She thought she'd heard something about his wife and that they'd enjoyed being together. Had the woman died, or due to age, gone into a home? Sage couldn't remember. But as she watched Norman, Sage understood that it took very little to remind someone of things loved -a smell, a food, a place.

"Mr. Stevens, is there anything else I can get you?" Sage interrupted his reverie, her own grief gnawing inside.

The elderly man looked at Sage with rheumy old eyes, probably once a gorgeous blue but now more the muted colors of pewter and periwinkle.

"Chili." he clinked his spoon to the rim of the bowl. "My wife made the best in town. Usually won a blue ribbon at the fair. Yes, it did. I haven't enjoyed a bowl of real chili for ages." He turned and found a place at one of the empty tables, taste-testing once, then eating heartily.

Sage had to swallow the lump of grief inside, for him or herself, she didn't know. She took a deep breath to choke off the tears that threatened.

"This smells mighty good, Miss Sage." Dakota Hayes, Eric's favorite writer and the reason Thistle Dew saved a weekend for a writer's conference, waited politely. "Your friend, Lowell, met us at the barns for a brief lesson on alpacas. They certainly are amazing creatures. It was interesting to learn that they are capable of generating affection much like horses." The young man had a handsome smile.

Sage shook off her melancholy thoughts and slipped into hostess mode, tucking her grief away to be dragged out later, when she was alone. She smiled brightly.

"They each have a distinct personality. Have you

15

met Chakra yet?" She asked. "He's the alpha male and the king of his domain. He has a real attitude problem but his offspring have a nice thick fleece and beautiful colorings." She quickly added, "I wasn't aware that Lowell was here today."

"Last I saw, he was helping your little girl, Paula is it - feed one of the baby animals." Maribelle offered as she picked through a vegetable platter and spooned French onion dip onto a small dish. "I think she called it 'Poop'."

"My daughter's name is Pia. And I sent her out with a bowl of apple peelings to feed her baby alpaca, Pooh," Sage turned toward the door. "I'll just be a minute."

Sage walked out back to the barns, oblivious of the cold, in search of her daughter. She had been trying to allow Pia a little more freedom to go to the barns, so why did her stomach feel as if she ate green apples? Her heart raced. Sage worked to control her panic with deep breaths as the therapist taught her many years ago. Her greatest challenge as Pia got older and more independent was to not transfer her own fears to her child. Inhaling the cold air helped to wash away her trepidation.

Sage rushed to enter the barn and was relieved to hear her daughter's sweet voice.

"Uncle Lowell, when will Daddy be done playing golf?"

Sage paused by the barn door, dread churning her stomach. She quietly watched as Pia and Lowell talked.

The little girl buried her face into the soft neck fur of her alpaca, Pooh. The baby animal responded by chewing on the end of one of her curly pig tails, untying a pink ribbon in the process.

"What did your Momma tell you?" Lowell mucked Chakra's stall. He paused to listen, leaning on the shovel to wait for the child's reply.

Sage's heart broke as she watched Pia's chin quiver. "She said Daddy won't be coming home anymore. He's in Heaven playing golf forever on a perfect course on a sunny day."

Lowell chuckled. "Your Momma's right, little girl. Your Daddy's on that putting green in the sky."

"Uncle Lowell, you silly, the sky is blue, not green." She giggled then continued somberly, "But Daddy promised he'd never leave Momma and me."

Pia left Pooh to stand on the bottom slat in order to peek between stalls.

"He promised, Uncle Lowell."

"Well, he asked me to help out whenever he was away. So, here I am. Here for you and your Mom." Lowell tossed a shovel full of dirty wood shavings into the wheelbarrow.

Chakra took that moment to lean into the stall and playfully nip Lowell on the shoulder.

"Dammit!" Lowell yelled as he jumped away from the alpaca while vigorously rubbing the bruise.

"Uh-oh, you said a bad word." Pia's eyes widened and she covered her ears with her hands.

Suddenly a tinkling sound caused them to look in the same direction. The copper wind chimes, that Eric had made from scraps after remodeling the bathrooms, quivered.

Sage felt the hairs on the back of her neck rise. The chimes seemed to sound even without the wind. Spiritual fingers? Eric?

"It sounds like the window is getting tickled." Pia giggled.

Lowell looked for an open window or source for the movement. "Dammit."

So Lowell felt something too. Sage brushed away a half-formed thought. Eric was gone. He couldn't make chimes move. He couldn't do anything. She squashed the ghostly little seed attempting to flourish in her mind.

"That's not nice, Uncle Lowell." Pia admonished Lowell. "And Daddy says words like that are bad."

"Well, your Daddy was right about that. Swear words are bad."

Sage decided it was time to enter the barn.

"Here you are, Sweet Pea, late for lunch." She picked the little girl up and hugged her. "How did Pooh like his apple peels?"

"He loved them. He said he'd like some more."

"Lowell, the animals look great. Thank you."

"Welcome." Lowell seemed pleased. He whistled as he returned to his task.

Sage carried Pia along the leaf littered path towards the house. "Tomorrow then, I guess our guests would like our famous apple cake with fresh vanilla ice cream." She nuzzled Pia's neck to make her giggle.

"Homemade?" Usually they only made their own ice cream for the Fourth of July picnic.

"Well, it's a lot of work. I couldn't do it alone."

"I know how." Pia put a hand on each side of her mother's face and stared into her eyes, "Can I do it?"

"Of course." Sage laughed as she put Pia down when they reached the back porch. "I certainly can't be expected to do all the cooking by myself."

"You need me." Pia smiled proudly, "Right, Mommy?"

"I sure do. I couldn't run this business without you, Sweet Pea."

They entered the warm kitchen. The muted laughter and conversation of the guests enjoying their lunches greeted them as Sage washed her hands and went about making bread for dinner.

"Don't we need Daddy, too?" Pia climbed up onto a stool by the pastry counter. "You told him that you can't run this business without him. Remember? On that day, Momma? The bad day when you told him that..."

18

Sage had to interrupt before she broke down in tears.

"I remember, Sweet Pea, but I guess Daddy knew we could do this ourselves. You and I. We're his special girls. Right?" Sage swallowed to keep the tremor from her voice. Tears burned her eyes, but she refused to let them fall. Not now, not now! She pounded the rising bread dough with more punch than necessary. Anger sometimes reared its ugly head when she least expected it.

"Right." Pia tried to retie her slimy, wet pink ribbons. "So is Uncle Lowell taking his place?" Finally, she yanked her ribbons from both pig tails.

Sage brought a warm soapy dishcloth to Pia and cleaned her little fingers.

"No." Sage answered quickly. "I mean it's very kind of him to help us out with the outdoor chores now and then, but no, he is not taking Daddy's place." Not in this lifetime.

Sage looked at Pia"s blue eyes. Eric's eyes. Every time she turned around today, it seemed she was reminded of Eric. Would the pain ever stop?

"Daddy will always be with us in spirit." She murmured past the lump in her throat.

"Like a ghost?" Pia asked, "I'm a-scared of ghosts."

"Not a ghost. But he's invisible. We can't see him or hear him. We just know he's here."

"We can feel him in here." Pia rubbed her chest with her right hand. "And hear him in our brain too. Right, Mommy? Sometimes Daddy is in my dreams. He whispers that he loves me."

Sage felt tightness in her chest, a painful tightness that could only be relieved by one of Eric's tender hugs. "Me too." She whispered and wrapped arms around her daughter and kissed her forehead. It was enlightening to finally admit it. Maybe Pia wasn't delusional after all. Maybe Pia was just a little girl who easily accepted those tingly moments for what they were. Her Daddy.

Sage tried not to think about the times she felt Eric's presence in the kitchen or while she was walking along the path through the woods to the pond. Sometimes she felt as if Eric was watching her, playing games or hiding behind a tree. She would stop and wait hoping to catch a glimpse of him or hear his infectious laugh - a misty sound, lately difficult to distinguish beneath the obnoxious cawing of hungry crows. She smiled longingly as memories danced behind her eyes. At first, she didn't see Hawke standing awkwardly at the kitchen door with an empty bread tray in his hand.

Sage saw the movement in her peripheral vision. She immediately swallowed her emotions, smiled politely at the man as she crossed the kitchen to slice another loaf of still warm bread and motioned for him to place the tray on the counter. How long had he been standing there?

"I'm sorry I interrupted your conversation." He did not smile, but a dimple revealed itself on his right cheek. His strong, lean face was clean shaven save for a neatly trimmed mustache. His thick, dark, shoulder length hair was pulled back and tied with a thin rawhide boot lace.

Why, on a day when she seemed to feel Eric every time she moved, did this man seem to always be around on the heels of those feelings? Was Eric trying to...stop, Sage. Stop now. Eric is dead. Ghosts aren't matchmakers, despite the movies.

She forced a smile as she refilled the tray. He touched her arm. The heat from his fingers was soothing but she shivered as if with a sudden chill.

"The chili is delicious. Again, I apologize for imposing on your private space."

Hawke left the kitchen. Sage expelled a breath she hadn't realized she was holding. She leaned against the counter to steady her shaking knees, twisted the dish cloth to quell her trembling hands. She closed her eyes and breathed deeply, working to control her racing heartbeat, the same familiar pace she experienced during a panic attack. Inhale count of four, exhale count of four. Heat, warm and comforting washed over her face. When she opened her eyes she squinted as a bright beam of sunshine streamed in through her window. The warm sun made her smile. The chimes moved in a delicate motion.

She dried Pia's hands and served her a small bowl of mild chili with cheese, a handful of crackers and a pink plastic princess glass of milk.

"How is it? Is there anything Mommy forgot?"

Sage watched Pia taste the chili with the aplomb of a seasoned television chef. Her mouth puckered and thinned as she tested the flavors with her tongue and smiled. Sage grinned. Being the official taster was an important job and Pia took her work seriously.

"Did you add the magic 'gredients?"

"Don't you taste them?"

They played this game with each entree.

Sage tasted a spoonful of chili. She hadn't been hungry since Eric died, hadn't done more than nibble. But this tasted pretty good. She had another spoonful and another.

Delicious, he had said. Yes, she thought, he was. Now where did THAT come from? The delicious chili. Hot and spicy. Tasty. Flavors toyed with her tongue. Fiery. A burn not unbearable caressed her mouth, and she suddenly awoke with need for more. Heat. Hawke's face flashed before her. She imagined him savoring her chili. She imagined him savoring...her.

Sage grabbed Pia's cold glass of milk and drank from it in an attempt to put out the fire.

"Very magic ingredients, indeed."

Pia covered her bowl with both hands. "Mommy, get your own bowl."

Sage laughed for the first time in ages. She filled a bowl and set it on the counter to cool.

"I'll go check the guests and then be back to have lunch with you, Sweet Pea."

"Okay." Pia stuffed a cracker in her mouth and grinned around the crumbs.

Sage went into the dining room and scanned the sideboard and then the room.

To check on Hawke.

Satisfied there was enough of everything, satisfied that Hawke was oblivious of the effect he had on her, she returned to the kitchen.

She settled on the stool and took time to enjoy being with her daughter.

"I like Mr. Norman." Pia shared with a mouthful of lunch. "He tells funny stories."

"Sweet Pea, swallow first." Sage poured a glass of milk. "What kind of stories?"

"Bout when he was a little boy in the golden days." Pia wiped her mouth with a paper napkin. "He had a dog named Laddie." She climbed down from her seat at the counter. "They had 'ventures."

"Adventures." Sage corrected, "Yes, he is a nice man." Pia let her mother wash her up and lead her to their private rooms behind the kitchen.

With lungs full of fresh autumn air, a full tummy and a soft blanket, it took less than one song for Pia to nap.

Sage fought the strong desire to cuddle up next to her child and sleep too, for just an hour. But duty called.

It wasn't until she was up to her elbows in soapsuds that her mother phoned. Audrey Jordan called every day. Audrey knew the monumental void Eric's death had created in Sage's life.

Eric was Sage's hero. From the day he saved her

from being kidnapped he'd been her champion. Eric was the only male Sage ever trusted besides her Dad.

Sage held the phone to one ear with her shoulder while she layered the ricotta and lasagna for the evening meal. Lowell entered the kitchen, ruddy faced, rubbing warmth into his hands. "Got any coffee?" He sat at the counter. "The critters are settled. I fixed Chakra's stall door."

"Thank you." Sage mouthed, listening to Audrey's voice in her ear.

"Got sugar?" Lowell asked.

Sage exaggerated the effort it took to slide the sugar bowl the approximately six inches to touch his mug.

"No, there are only seven guests here now. Tomorrow there should be around thirty or so." She told Audrey.

"Cream?" Lowell interrupted once again.

She flashed him a stern frown.

"Lunch? Yes. That would be lovely, Mom. It'll give Pia a chance to wear the new dress you bought her." Sage put the finishing touches on the lasagna. "We'll see you then. Take care. Bye Mom." She returned the phone to its cradle, then calmly carried first one, then another heavy pan to the oven. She turned to him.

"Lowell, that was rude."

"You're right about that! You should have hung up when I came in." He dunked a chocolate chip cookie into his coffee and slurped as he ate it.

"Pardon me?" She couldn't believe his audacity. "This is my kitchen, MY home, and that was Eric's mother on the phone."

"Yeah, and I just came in from doin' Eric's work. He was my best friend too! You seem to forget that." He spat coffee with cookie crumbs onto the counter as he spoke. His face, already reddened from the cold, brightened with anger. "The least you could do is remember THAT!"

She exhaled. He was here, helping with the yard and barn chores. She could be polite.

"You're right Lowell. I'm sorry. Thank you for your help."

From the beginning, he refused payment for the work, had actually been insulted when she'd offered him money. Although she was grateful for his help, she hated being obligated to him. To anyone. But especially to him.

"Would you like a bowl of hot chili and some fresh bread?"

"Now that's more like it." He looked smug. "For now."

****

The melody of the lunch triangle reminded Eric about his broken thumb. At least it didn't hurt in cold weather anymore. He shimmered with pride at the way Sage handled everything lately, although he ached watching her try not to cry. She was being so strong.

And Lowell. What's going on with you? I know what you're thinking, old friend. You've always had a thing for Sage, I know, but trust me, pal, you're a friend. That's all. I know you wondered if it was me making the wind chimes jingle. It was. And I asked Chakra to nip you, too. Just as a little reminder to keep your place. Hands off my wife!

The sound of Sage laughing with Pia during lunch made his soul rejoice. "That's my girl. I've missed that sound." Eric flew around the room causing the curtains to ruffle. "One tiny step toward healing."

He sat on the foot of the bed when Sage sang to Pia at naptime. "You are such a good mother, Sage." He reached out to touch her. "You were such a good wife." Diamond teardrops clouded Eric's vision.

Chapter 3

By nine o'clock the following morning, there were thirty-seven writers crowded in the great room sipping coffee, sharing tales and enjoying warm blueberry muffins and an apple crumb cake. A fire crackled and hissed in the large granite fireplace though its comforting sounds were lost amid the imaginative discourse playing tag among the gathering.

Pia was snuggled up to Norman as he spoke to a couple of aspiring authors. She played with the watch she mischievously stole from his wrist after discovering a button that illuminated the face.

Sage moved from group to group to refill beverages. Earlier she'd strategically placed some simple snack trays so the guests could help themselves. Most were empty now, but she knew by the time she'd refilled drinks it'd be time to set out more. Food was pretty much continuous when she had guests, between the meals and snacks. She was grateful for that fact, as it kept her too busy to think. To grieve.

Hawke looked gorgeous in the black T-shirt and gray blazer he wore with snug fitting jeans. Sage studied his full lips as he spoke, and grinned as he bit his lower lip when thinking. She decided he was probably a very good kisser.

He glanced at her and winked.

Her face heated up and she was unable to look away. Thankful he couldn't read minds, she broke eye-contact and continued around the room.

Sage saw Hawke and a sexy interviewer laugh

and bring their heads together as if sharing a secret. She inhaled and unconsciously held her breath. Their images blurred. She released her breath in an audible sigh.

Slowly she worked her way to their group, trying to rein in her wayward body's sudden awakening.

"Mrs. Winters." Hawke shifted his position on the loveseat and motioned for her to join the small crowd. "I wonder if you'd answer a question."

Sage knew her place at this retreat, hostess, only hostess, not participant but as much as she knew she should not join them, she justified her compliance as an act of courtesy.

"I'm not a writer, Mr. Hawke. I'm not sure I can help you."

"May I have a refill?" A woman asked, holding her cup and saucer out for Sage.

Sage automatically filled the woman's cup and gave a nervous smile to the group. She set the nearly empty pot on a nearby table.

"Only a minute of your time." Hawke indicated the place beside him. Sage sat in the space beside Hawke with her trembling hands safely tucked between her knees.

Hawke read a passage from his latest work-in-progress. "My character's reaction has been questioned. What do you think, as a parent, have I missed something?"

Sage glanced at the others who appeared to be interested in her reply, save for a woman dressed in a designer slacks ensemble, who suggestively toyed with a large fiery opal necklace nestled in the space just above the neckline of her ivory lace camisole. The woman leaned forward allowing Hawke a clear view of cleavage.

"Well," Sage couldn't think. She shifted to the edge of the cushion so the heat from Hawke's shoulder couldn't melt her brain. "I do know that panic is a powerful force, it seems to control all other emotions and thoughts." Sage felt that same feeling creep into her body as she spoke.

Panic. Not about Pia this time.

What was it?

She couldn't place it. Her heart raced like a panic attack. A reaction Sage related to fear. What was she afraid of? She looked across the room at Pia, contentedly playing with Norman's watch. It wasn't her customary fears. This was something unfamiliar. She had to go. Needed to be in the kitchen, away from everyone, so she could breathe. Away from Hawke, so she could breathe.

"Are you all right?" His velvety voice and gentle touch on her shoulder communicated his concern.

"I just remembered something in the oven." She lied and jumped up. Her body mourned the loss of his warming closeness. Dear God, what was she thinking?

She hurried into the kitchen. She was leaning against the counter, trying to steady her heartbeat when Pia walked in. Norman's watch dangled from her tiny wrist.

"Know what time it is?" Pia studied the clock face, her little face scrunched up with concentration.

Sage was just about to say that it was almost noon when Pia announce "Its snack time."

"Already?"

Pia pointed to the watch and nodded. "Mr. Norman told me."

Minutes later Pia carried a bowl of her favorite crunchy granola treat out to the guests. Sage followed with the coffee carafe.

"What is this?" Hawke asked as he tasted a small handful of the concoction Pia held out. "MMMMMMM. Delicious." Hawke caught Sage's eye. "Delicious."

Sage tried to ignore the fluttering in her stomach. Maybe she was hungry. Maybe she was coming down with the flu. Maybe she was beginning to like a little flirtation from Hawke.

"It's Puppy Chow. Momma makes it. She says it's a healthy snack."

To Pia's delight Puppy Chow was a hit with the adults. Sage brought out small baskets with grapes and cherries to each group then made the rounds refilling coffee and teacups while Pia carried a small tray with cream and sugar.

Satisfied that the guests were all temporarily cared for, mother and daughter set up the buffet table for the last meal of this gathering. Pia lined up the utensils, made a neat display of linen napkins and then carried out a stack of wooden salad bowls. Sage followed with a huge bowl of leafy greens, cheese and croutons.

"I didn't think you could top the chili," Norman complimented, "but something smells mighty good coming from the kitchen."

"Lunch will be served shortly." Sage offered, pleased with Norman's comment.

The Italian buffet of spinach lasagna, linguini with white clam sauce and pumpkin ravioli with a sage butter sauce appeared to be a hit.

"Ms. Winters will you marry me?" Dakota teased as he heaped another helping onto his plate.

"No, she's gonna marry me." Another voice called out. Sage felt a rush of color creep into her face. Who said that?

Was it Hawke?

She turned to see Lowell standing in the doorway, wearing his overalls and muck covered boots.

Sage had a sudden burning anger. Lowell thought he could simply claim her as his own? She'd rebuffed his hints before. What had her guests thought? That Lowell and she would be together at some point? She looked around the room.

Hawke stared at her for a second then simply looked down at his empty plate.

Sage pushed past Lowell knowing he would follow.

"What are you doing? You are NOT to go into the great room especially with those on." She quietly berated and directed him out the back door.

"I know, but I heard that conversation and didn't want anyone bothering you."

"They are paying guests, Lowell. He was simply teasing and I took it as such. I don't need anyone to champion me." Sage heard herself say the words and thought about Eric, her champion. Eric, now gone. Oh, Eric...she stopped the thought.

"I was only trying to help." Lowell's tone was bitter.

"I know, Lowell." Sage sighed. She couldn't afford to lose him. He was helping her without payment. "Thank you."

"I'll go about my chores now," he said it gruffly, but his expression was mollified.

As afternoon crept closer, Sage called Pia to lunch, then took the child to their rooms for her nap.

Pia gathered three of her favorite picture books and climbed up on her bed to settle down.

Sage sat on the edge of the bed as always, reached for a book and began to read.

"Mommy, can Mr. Norman read to me today? He said *Charlotte's Web* was his little girl's favorite story too and he hasn't read it for a very long time."

"Oh." Sage hesitated. "Well. Sure. I'll go ask him. But he might be busy with the other writers, you know?"

Sage found Norman alone on the porch, puffing his pipe. He was thrilled with Pia's invitation, stuck his smoldering pipe into his pocket of his cardigan and followed Sage to the private rooms behind the kitchen.

The old man sat in a rocking chair and patted his knee. Pia climbed onto his lap with purple bunny and fell asleep before he finished the first chapter.

When Sage peeked in on them, Pia was snuggled on Norman's lap as he rocked slowly, both lost in contented sleep. As Sage attempted to cover them with a quilt, Norman woke and together they carefully put Pia to bed.

"Thank you." The old man glowed as they stood at the counter in the kitchen. "I think reading to Pia was the high point of my weekend."

Sage leaned in and kissed his cheek.

"It was probably Pia's favorite story time in a long while too."

Sage took the quiet time to wrap up leftovers and clean up the kitchen. She made herself a plate of ravioli, one of Eric's favorite meals, and sat at the counter to eat her lunch.

"Eating alone?" Hawke stood at the swing doors. "That's just not right."

"It's okay." She stood, "What can I get for you?"

"A glass of water, please." He stepped inside the room letting the doors close behind him. "I can get it. You can finish your lunch."

"Thanks." She sat back down, "The glasses are in the cupboard to the left."

He had his back to her as he let the water run to cold for a minute, then filled his glass. She studied his broad shoulders, trim waist and especially liked how his jeans fit him.

"Are you into biking? A bicycle I mean. For exercise."

He turned, leaned his bicycle butt against the sink and slowly drank the water.

She became mesmerized by the movement of his Adam's apple as he swallowed. There was nothing sexy about an Adam's apple but she couldn't look away.

"Yes, I bike." He placed the empty glass in the sink. "And jog."

It shows, she thought and felt pink heat her face.

He gave her a grin, as if he knew she was ogling his butt. "I got into biking a year ago. This year I qualified for a one hundred mile bike tour that raises money for Missing and Exploited Children. It really pushed me."

"I've read about that tour." Sage was impressed.

Someone called his name from the great room.

"Duty calls." He said, still smiling as he went through the door.

That dimple. That body. Sage mentally shook herself and sternly warned against wool-gathering. Looking around the bright kitchen, she realized that everything was done.

And her plate was empty. She stared, surprised she'd eaten it all.

Where had the time gone?

Pia, Sage thought suddenly, has been napping too long; the fresh air and good company must have exhausted her. The subtle shiver of fear crept in and washed through her body. Sage looked toward the apartment door. She felt an urgent need to check on her daughter.

Sage hurried as the panic threatened.

"Pia, Sweet Pea, time to wake up. What a long nap you've taken!" Finding the twin bed in Pia's room empty, Sage went to her own bedroom, but there was no sign of Pia there either.

"Pia," she called as she checked in the closets and under the beds. "Pia, Sweet Pea, our guests are leaving and they would like to say good bye to you."

Surely, the promise of attention would bring Pia out, especially since she took her responsibilities as hostess helper so very seriously. However, Pia did not appear.

Okay. Sage took a deep, centering breath. She was in control here, not her emotions. A critical eye confirmed that Pia was not in the apartment.

Sage studied the scene in Pia's room. Pia's sweater was missing from the back of the chair and her sneakers no longer rested on the mat by the door. Pia had gone outside without permission. She clenched her hands into fists then hurried through the kitchen and outside towards the barns with the mantra "She knows better, she knows better" echoing in her mind.

She met one of the writers on the path. "Mrs. Winters, I'm leaving now. I wanted to thank you for providing such an exceptional location for the writer's retreat."

Sage couldn't remember the man's name, her fear for Pia was so great.

"You're very welcome." Sage glanced around the yard, "You'll have to excuse me. Have you seen Pia?"

"Yes, I saw her running in that direction." The man pointed to the woods.

"Towards the pond?" Sage asked. "Alone?"

"Yes but I wouldn't worry. You know Hawke? He was sitting on its banks as we walked by."

Sage nodded. "Thank you. I'm glad you enjoyed your stay. Please excuse me, but I have to run."

Sage literally ran down the leaf littered path through the woods that led to Little Pond. She slowed as she caught sight of Pia.

And Hawke. Together.

He crouched beside her taking turns throwing bread to the mallard family who had adopted Little Pond as their home.

Pia looked small as she stood beside the broad shouldered man. Sage thought he looked ruggedly handsome and warm in the ivory fisherman knit sweater and wool scarf wrapped nonchalantly around his neck.

Pia giggled as her hands and bread got lost in the long sleeves of his aged brown leather bomber jacket.

Sage watched the tall man attempt to roll the sleeves up. But when he retrieved the prize bread from the inner depths of the sleeves, and handed it to Pia, they both threw back their heads in laughter. She swung her arm like a baseball player pitching and flung the wad of bread out to the impatient duck family.

Sage was startled to feel comforting warmth. She released fear's cold grip and smiled at the playful interaction. This was a good sign that Pia would survive the death of her father.

"Come on, little lady. I bet your mom is worried about you." Hawke stood to his full height, towering over the small blonde child. The breeze blew his long brown hair into his eyes.

She watched as he finger-combed his hair back, away from his face.

As Pia danced around him flapping her arms and quacking, Hawke chuckled, a low rumble that made Sage tingle.

She stared entranced until Pia's voice reminded her that she was a widow.

"Na uh." Pia paused in her dance and corrected him, "This is my yard. Mommy said, 'don't leave the yard.'"

"Let's go check on your mom then. To see everything is all right. I know you're her helper."

"I'll come back tomorrow, Lucky Duck." Pia waved.

Her little hand reached up trustingly to become enveloped in his much larger one. As they turned to walk back towards the house the duckling family complained raucously.

Not wanting it to appear that she had been watching the pair for a few minutes Sage took the opportunity to step forward just then.

"There you are, you little imp." Sage knelt and Pia ran and leapt into her mother's waiting hug with a giggle and a squeeze around her mother's neck.

"Lucky and his family were really hungry." She anxiously explained to her mother. "I remembered that I forgot to bring them bread yesterday." Pia leaned back and placed her tiny cold palms on Sage's cheeks and stared into her eyes.

"Isn't it our rule that you do not go to the pond alone?"

"No. Our rule is that I only go to the pond with you. But you were busy saying good-bye to all of the people. Lucky Duck 'spects me to be 'sponsible and feed him." The little girl logically justified her misbehavior. "And I was not alone 'cause I found Mr. Hawke just bein' lonely on the grass." Pia wiggled from her mother's hold and ran back a few steps to Hawke and once again took his hand. "We were coming to check if you needed my help. Weren't we, Mr. Hawke?"

Sage stood. "I hope she didn't make a nuisance of herself, Mr. Hawke." She reached out her hand for Pia. "She can talk the red off an apple."

"Pia is delightful company." Sage could see that he meant it. As their eyes met for that instant, Sage felt the racing beat in her chest. It mimicked a panic attack.

"I got cold so Mr. Hawke let me wear his jacket." Pia interrupted.

Sage closed her eyes to disconnect and struggled to look away. Her mind felt like scrambled eggs. She inhaled deeply, then with a clear head and a tiny grasp on her self control she looked down at Pia with a comforting smile.

The orange sunset reflected on the pond,

glittering gold in the ripples as the Lucky Duck family played follow the leader to settle for the night in the cattails along its edge. It was a moment Sage would have trouble shaking from her mind for many days.

****

This weekend has been such a success, Sage. The writers really enjoyed themselves. And I did too. I followed Dakota around and listened to his workshop. Man, I love his books. He's so much like me in his quest for adventure. I think that's why he's my favorite author.

I really loved watching the old guy, Norman, connect with Pia. I have to admit I got a little jealous listening to him read to her. That used to be my special time with our daughter. I was reading Charlotte's Web that spring of the accident. I didn't get to finish it. I hope she lets you read to her after the authors leave.

Sage, you don't have to panic so much when Pia is out of sight. I'm watching over her. I won't let anything happen to her. I promised a long time ago, remember? I promised to always take care of you. Both of you.

Chapter 4

The holidays passed dismally and in the heart of winter, Sage found she needed a man more than ever.

Lowell was good with the barn chores and even shoveled the walk reluctantly, but he was useless when something broke down. And right now the snow blower wouldn't start and the parking area needed to be cleared.

The writers were returning and Sage felt her heart flutter at the thought of having them come back. One in particular had a smile that kept popping into her head.

Sage watched her friend, Peter, as he listened to a call on his police radio. He was off duty today and had come at Sage's request to repair the snow blower. Peter was one of the foursome playing golf the day Eric was killed. Where Lowell came everyday to handle his grief, Peter stayed away.

"Do you have to leave?" Sage knew that in a small town with a small police department Peter was called often.

"No. Everything's fine. Mrs. Cabot was walking down the street in her bathrobe again. Danny took her home."

"Peter, thank you so much for your help."

"No problem, Sage." Peter rocked in the old porch chair as he sipped from the mug of steaming coffee. "The snow blower was barely working last winter. Eric and I talked about whether he should get it fixed or if he should invest in a new one. I thought he decided to get a new one. Guess he never

36

got around to it."

"I'm amazed it lasted this long." She laughed quietly. "We bought it at the Smith's yard sale when they retired to Florida. Like he said about everything he bought that needed repair, 'this'll do'." She chuckled, recalling the overpriced house she wanted to buy for their bed and breakfast, and the abandoned farm in desperate need of repair that he wanted. "This'll do," he decided. Then he went on to describe to her how beautiful it would be with a little work.

"These northeastern winters put a snow blower to the test, that's for sure. But let me plow it for you." Peter, in addition to his position as county sheriff, had a booming plowing business in the winter. "You don't need to worry about the snow in your parking lot."

The nearby chatter of some cardinals interrupted their conversation as the friends appreciated the moment. They watched the birds fly off into the trees.

"I can never get enough of this view." Peter looked out at the yards and pasture. "It sure is pretty. Norman Rockwell pretty."

"I love it too." Sage felt a rush of warmth. "Eric and I worked hard to get that look."

"God, I miss Eric. I'm sorry I haven't been around much since the accident."

Before she could answer, the phone rang inside. A few minutes later she returned with the coffeepot and refilled his mug.

"We're keeping the rooms filled at least. We're booked into March." She blushed, very pleased with herself. She had heard the talk in town, saying that she wouldn't be able to go it alone. She was more determined than ever to show them a thing or two.

"That's really great, Sage. How's my little goddaughter doing?" Peter asked, "I haven't seen Pia since our Christmas party."

"She's doing pretty well." Sage looked out across the expanse of white. "She'll be sorry to have missed your visit."

"Where is she?" He set his mug on a tree trunk that served as porch table. "I thought I might stay long enough to see her."

"She's with Lowell on the snowmobile packing down the cross country skiing trails." Sage's smile never quite reached her eyes. "I fixed them a picnic lunch. She'll be more than ready for a nap when they return. Last time she fell asleep on the ride back."

"And Lowell?" Peter asked. "Has he been...okay?"

She nodded. "He's been helpful." That surely minimized his daily self-imposed obligations. She added reluctantly, "More than that, he's been a blessing. I couldn't have opened up and kept the Inn going without his help."

"I'm sorry Sage." Peter took her hands in his. "I'm sorry I haven't been here for you. It's just that Eric and I...It's just that I...Ruthie called me a coward." His eyes watered. "Somehow I could pretend that it never happened if I stayed away." He sniffed and studied the floor intently. "I'm sorry."

Sage watched him and remembered the little boy who hid in the cellar of his dad's hardware store after his mom died and completely missed her funeral.

"I'm not a very good friend." He confessed. "Eric would have been there for Ruth if it had been me who..."

"Died," she said matter-of-factly. "I have an empty space too, Peter. A hole, huge and gaping right here." She pressed a hand to her chest. "Every morning when I get up I want to tell him about a dream that I had. I want to share the sunrise with him here on the porch and I can't. For the first few months after Eric's funeral I would set two mugs on the counter for our coffee. I would get so angry at myself for forgetting, so angry at him for leaving, so angry at myself for crying. Again. Every single day for months, Peter."

"I'm such a jerk, Sage. Acting as if I'm the one he left behind. I'm so sorry."

She leaned over and hugged him, "Eric loved you like a brother, Peter."

They sat there in quiet solitude for a long time sharing their pain, comforting each other, until he finally inhaled deeply.

"You're quite a woman, Sage." He finished his coffee with one last swig and stood to leave. "Ruth asked me to invite you and Pia to dinner on Thursday. She said you have a high school girl working the desk part time after school."

Sage rose and together they walked towards his car. "I'm still training her, but I think it will be good to let her be on her own for an hour or two."

Peter pointed to the top of a utility pole. "Hey, look. A hawk."

Sage felt her heart skip a beat as her eyes swept across the parking area, then followed his gesture to see the magnificent bird swoop from its perch and disappear to the woods behind the barns.

"He must have spotted a field mouse or something."

Speechless, Sage only nodded, inwardly chastising her body for the wash of heat that coursed through it.

"We'll see you on Thursday. Pia misses you."

He kissed her cheek and climbed into his car.

Sage waved as he backed out of the driveway. She turned quickly back to work, back to now, back to being alone. Back to forgetting Eric and remembering Hawke. No, that was wrong, she had it backwards. How could she ever forget her champion?

How could she forget the man who loved her so much he'd saved her life? Sage shut off her brain, despite the tight feeling in her chest. She mentally repeated the mantra that kept her going every day. *Pia needs me.*

In the time it took for Sage to refill the birdfeeders and hang a new ball of suet, she could hear the increasing roar of the snowmobile and waited until it stopped beside the shoveled walk.

"So, how's Pete?" Lowell stepped onto the porch cradling a sleeping Pia in his arms.

"He's fine. How'd you know he was here?" As Sage reached for Pia, Lowell took a step toward the door.

"I'll carry her in," he whispered. He nodded toward the tray with the two empty mugs on it. Oh, of course, that's how he knew. Only Pete used the *Have you hugged a cop today?* mug. She held the doors open for him and led him into the private quarters and Pia's bedroom where he gently laid her on her bed. Sage untied the wool hat from beneath her little chin and removed it.

"Hurry up." Lowell moved to the door. "I need some coffee."

Sage closed her eyes and breathed deeply waiting for her temper to relax. She worked slowly removing snowsuit and boots so as not to wake Pia and to let Lowell know that he could not order her around. Sage pulled the quilt over her daughter and signaled Lowell out of the room and then out into the kitchen.

Sage sighed deeply knowing in the common sense part of her brain that at some point soon, she would have to risk losing Lowell's friendship. And his help. Despite the fact that he worked around the property without pay, she finally admitted to herself that she'd rather pay for a hired hand than be obligated to Lowell unwillingly.

"How long ago did she fall asleep?" Sage handed Lowell a mug of coffee. "Did you eat lunch?"

"Yeah, we ate. She said the brownies needed more chocolate chips." He gulped down some of the hot brew and winced. "She also said your blueberry jelly isn't as sweet as your strawberry jelly. Personally, I really wished for a ham and cheese on rye not peanut butter, but you must take me for a four year old."

Sage held calm. Where was the thank you? She was searching for something clever to say but the tinkle of the bell at the front door announced the arrival of a guest. "Excuse me."

****

In the quiet afternoon, while Pia napped, Lowell worked in the barns and Kristen worked the front desk, Sage relished the peace and quiet of the kitchen as she baked some pies and organized the weekly menu. An unfamiliar call from outside interrupted her quietude. She gazed out the window, had to lean over the sink to search the sky and nearby trees for the source of the eerie cry. And there, at the top of the utility pole a hawk, was it the same hawk? perched, watching, waiting. Sage laughed nervously and returned to her task, glancing again to see the hawk resting on the pole. A hawk. She shivered.

Hawke.

By dusk almost all of the guests had checked in and were gathering amicably in the great room. The house once again bubbled with conversation and laughter. Sage loved the sound. And it kept her mind too busy to focus on the image of Hawke. Where was he? Maybe he was chronically late. His one flaw. Good. At least he wasn't totally perfect.

Sage was tall, but she imagined her shoulder would fit comfortably under his arm. Perhaps his dark chocolate hair needed a trim by some standards, but Sage discovered that his shaggy look really made her stomach flutter. His eyes seemed to have the capacity to read her soul; a thought that both completely unnerved her and comforted her simultaneously.

Sage looked for the hawk again and was disappointed that the perch was vacant. She breathed deeply, needing a zen moment.

She peeked into the great room to see the guests visiting.

Sage caught a glimpse of the last writer as he checked in at the desk, complimenting Kristen on her efficiency at holding his reservation despite his late arrival. Sage let the swing door almost closed, but watched fascinated as Kristen blushed and giggled during their brief dialogue. He looked good.

Sage let her gaze travel down his athletic form. Whew, he certainly must work out all winter. Those jeans fit him so snug, she smiled as she imagined slipping her hand into his back pocket as they walked side-by-side.

Then, in her imagination they wandered to a place where they stopped walking, he would turn to her and placed his gentle palm on her cheek, letting the sensuous pad of his thumb, trace her quivering lips.

She licked her lips and nearly fell backwards when a quick glance at his smiling face alerted her that she'd been caught in her daydream. The swing door bumped her forehead as she retreated into the safety of her kitchen. My goodness, what am I doing? Sage sat on the counter stool, elbows on the counter, head in her hands in an effort to regain her composure.

As if on cue, Lowell blew in through the back door with a frigid burst of air. "Gawd almighty! It's cold out there. The temperature must've dropped thirty degrees in the past hour." He rubbed his gloved hands together. "Things should be all set for the week." He removed his gloves and blew warm breath on his fingers.

Sage handed him a mug of hot coffee. "Thank you, Lowell."

"Yeah." He gruffly replied as he made himself comfortable at the counter. "Full house tonight?"

She stood and took a pie from the oven to set it on a cooling rack. "Yes. No vacancies. Isn't that awesome?"

"Yeah." He sipped the steamy brew, "Freakin' awesome."

"Mommy." A little raspy voice called from the private quarters. Pia shuffled into the kitchen all tousled from her long nap. Sage scooped Pia up into a hug and smoothed the fly away curls from her face. "Well, good evening, sleepy head. Did you have sweet dreams?"

"Uh huh." Pia nodded. "Me and Pooh had a 'venture." Sage sat Pia on the counter and got her a glass of water.

"Hi Uncle Lowell." Pia took a few gulps and set her glass down next to Lowell's mug. "We had fun working today, didn't we? We had a pic-a-nic, didn't we?"

"We sure did."

"I made yellow snow." Pia giggled.

At Sage's glare Lowell quickly offered, "It was an emergency. We were too far away from the house to get back here in time."

Pia nodded. "But I can't write my name like Uncle Lowell told me Daddy and him used to do." She added matter-of-factly, "Girls can't."

Lowell turned away from Sage's disapproving scowl, "Did you tell your Mom that you drove part of the way?"

"What? Lowell. No." Sage panicked, envisioning the sled running into a tree or swallowed up by the pond. She quickly put Pia on the floor. "Sweet Pea, do you know who came today? Do you remember your friend Mr. Norman? I think he's out in the great room."

Pia eyes widened as she remembered the kind old man who read her stories. She rushed to the door then paused, "I was very careful steering the snowmobile, Mommy. Wasn't I, Uncle Lowell?"

"You sure were, Princess." He actually sounded proud of her.

After Pia left the room Sage turned to Lowell. "Are you crazy?! Lowell, she's four years old. FOUR. What were you thinking?" Sage kept her voice just above a whisper to keep from screaming at him.

"Calm down, Sage." He grabbed her arm. "Do you seriously think I would ever put Pia in danger?" His grip became painful, "God, Sage, Pia is like a daughter to me. I would never hurt her." He released Sage and turned away. "I could hate you for not trusting me." He paced the kitchen. "I would give my life for you. For both of you. Don't you know that?" He pounded his fist against the door frame, rattling the window. Sage had never seen him this angry.

"Lowell, you just don't think." Sage kept the counter island between them. "She's only four."

Lowell stood, his hands clenched by his sides. "I would never put her in danger."

"Lowell." Sage reminded him, "You gave her a tarantula for Christmas."

"How could I know she'd carry on like she did?"

It had been a horrible morning as Sage tried to calm her terrified daughter.

"I thought she would like it. She cried when the old man read her the part where the spider died. I thought she'd like a pet spider."

"Lowell," Sage poured herself a glass of milk. "A spider is a little thing that spins a web in the barn." Sage desperately wanted something stronger to drink, but she and Eric never kept liquor in the house. Without thinking, she said aloud, "You never cease to amaze me at how clueless you are sometimes."

Lowell stepped back as if he'd been slapped. "That's cruel, Sage." He looked sincerely crushed. "I really do care about you and Pia." His eyes glistened as he silently zipped his jacket and put his gloves on. He stormed out of the house. "I promise you'll regret that."

****

What were YOU thinking, Sage? Now you've gone and gotten Lowell so mad he'll sit around and pout at home for days. Who will help you now?

Eric followed as Lowell stormed out of the house to the barns. He chuckled as he eavesdropped on Lowell's mumbling while he mucked stalls.

"Damn animals. You're just a hungry bunch of ugly creatures who eat too much and are of no use."

Eric grinned.

Lowell spread wood shavings. "Horses I can understand. People ride them. Cows provided milk or steak. Chickens even provide eggs and barbecue wings."

Then Lowell scooped their rations of feed. "But you little camel-looking things have no purpose but to keep men annoyingly busy. You are a bunch of sorry critters."

The black male, Chakra, turned from him and released an audible and offensive smelling burst of gas.

Lowell cussed at the animal and punched him on the hind end.

Eric burst out laughing and watched Lowell jump as the barn door slammed in a sudden gust of wind.

Sage, did he tell you what Chakra did? I swear that animal is smarter than a fifth grader. And

Lowell isn't. I almost fell right off my cloud he got me laughing so hard. Pia wasn't in any danger with Lowell on the snowmobile. I was with her. I'll keep her safe.

Promise.

Chapter 5

It was another dreary morning in February. Cold breezes caused leafless bush branches to brush against her bedroom window with an eerie scratching, reminding Sage of her old math teacher, Miss Hannifer, scraping chalk on the blackboard.

Eric's funny faces, gestures and mischievous smiles always made her giggle as they watched Miss Hannifer's sagging arm flesh wiggle as she wrote out equations.

"Eric remember..." she spoke aloud instinctively turning toward the bed's center.

But his space in their bed was empty, and the sheets had been laundered so many times that there was no longer a lingering trace of his scent. In the beginning, when she realized that she couldn't smell him in bed anymore she sprinkled his pillow with the cologne she got him on his last birthday. But it wasn't the same.

One night in desperation she rubbed his deodorant on the pillowcase. That was the worst. She sobbed at the lost of his smell. Eric never smelled like anything store bought. It would be impossible to duplicate his presence with cologne.

Although time brought back rational thought, built strength and re-established calm, Sage still blinked back tears. Isn't it funny, she mused with resolve, that sometimes she desperately missed his smell of all things?

Sage shuddered, bopped the buzzing alarm button, snuggled beneath the covers and closed her eyes tight momentarily blocking out her life without

Eric. She remembered Eric's teasing that she should have a Bed and Lunch since she had never been a morning person.

In the beginning Eric made the breakfasts for their guests while she washed dishes and changed the bedding. They slipped into a comfortable routine with the bulk of their work being done by noon. The writer's retreat though was a whole different ball game. Breakfast, snacks and evening meals were included in the retreat package.

Eric loved watching the sun rise. He would wake up bright eyed at the crack of dawn, whip up a batch of blueberry pancakes from scratch and wonder why his girl didn't appreciate his six o'clock wake up call.

"Ugh…" Sage sighed aloud.

Since Eric died, it was imperative that Sage become an early riser for the sake of their business. But it didn't mean she had to suddenly love mornings.

Thank goodness the coffeemaker turned on automatically. When she remembered the previous evening, she was gratefully rewarded with a hot cup of fresh brewed coffee.

In the beginning, in those first weeks after she decided to keep Thistle Dew opened, Ruthie stepped in and cooked breakfast for the guests with a hidden agenda to teach Sage numerous breakfast recipes. It became clear to Ruthie after only a few weeks that once Sage had a hot shower and a cup of coffee she could whip up a variety of delicious morning meals to satisfy the appetites of even the fussiest guests.

Sage could just imagine Eric tasting her cinnamon French Toast or Citrus Ambrosia, hesitant at first, but then actually enjoying it and complimenting her with "this'll do."

Her breakfast menu was simple and country, with a touch of lumberjack just the way Eric would have wanted it. Bacon, ham or sausage links, flapjacks, waffles or French toast, with homemade maple syrup. Sage added pancakes with strawberries and whipped cream and bagels and English muffins with an assortment of flavored cream cheeses.

If she could help it no one left for a day of skiing or skating or shopping on an empty stomach.

Their original agreement for management of the bed and breakfast had been that Sage would tend to the housekeeping and bookkeeping while Eric would see to breakfasts and the outdoor chores. So much for best laid plans. Sage's frustration and grief suffocated her so she breathed in slowly and deeply then exhaled slowly and deeply until she felt in control once again.

The persistent buzzer interrupted her thoughts and she grudgingly climbed out of bed to begin her day.

Coffee, she thought, before anything else, coffee. Barely functioning through her fuzzy-brain, she padded through the small living room, slowly opened Pia's bedroom door and peeked in. Her pixie child slept soundly, curled up like a kitten on her pillow, her purple bunny cuddled tightly under her chin.

"All is well." Sage whispered as she entered the dark kitchen. She flipped on the lights while repeating the mantra, "One day at a time, Sage." She stared at the empty coffeemaker. She forgot to get it ready last night. Darn!

As she filled the coffeepot with water she reiterated, "You just have to make it through one day at a time."

"Can I help with something?"

Sage gasped and dropped the half filled pot which shattered against the stainless steel sink.

At the swing door, Hawke stood holding his empty coffee mug like a panhandler on the corner of a busy intersection. His cheeks reddened and he hurried to her side at the sink.

"You're not cut are you?" He held her hands, searching for a sign of injury. "I'm truly sorry." His gentle touch sparked a flame within.

She pulled her hands away, wiped them on a dishtowel and sagged against the counter.

"I only hoped for some coffee." He spoke apologetically.

She only stared at him, assimilating the events of the past three seconds, trying to make her body move, to do something, to make some comment, to do anything. But the order of her daily routine, the mechanical method with which she started each and every day, had been completely sabotaged by this intruder. This amazingly handsome, cleft chinned, scruffy faced intruder.

She couldn't think. Couldn't make her way through the too- early-in-the-morning foggy brain, the I-haven't-had-my-first-cup-of-coffee brain, the this-man-makes-me-giddy brain.

"I'll pick up the glass out of the sink." He pulled off some paper towels and began the task. "I didn't mean to startle you."

She was thankful she hadn't responded with a blood curdling scream that would have awakened the whole house. Despite her rapidly pounding heart and the thundering in her ears, she calmly went to the pantry, climbed on the stepping stool, retrieved a box from the top shelf, then opened the package to reveal a brand new coffee pot.

His responding grin almost caused her to drop this one too, but she set it beside the sink.

She began grinding the whole beans, pretending to be in total control.

He washed and rinsed the new pot and then after filling it, poured it into the coffee maker.

"Thank you." Sage spoke tersely as she went to the refrigerator. "I apologize that there wasn't coffee available to you this morning. I didn't expect anyone to be up this early. Breakfast begins at seven."

"Actually, I haven't slept." He glanced over to the coffee which seemed to be dripping painfully slow.

She gave him a concerned look.

"I was writing." He said hastily.

She stared for long minutes and saw amusement quirk on his mouth. The man was entirely too cheerful for this time of day.

"You're not a morning person." He said and nodded sagely, obviously not expecting an answer. He sat on a stool by the center island and watched her retrieve two oblong pans, placing them in the oven.

"Breakfast strata." She spoke aloud and mentally checked that off her morning list of to-do's. If he sat here, she decided she'd attempt to be a hostess, even if he did know she wasn't a morning person.

"What is that?"

"Lots of good things mixed together like an omelet, but baked instead of fried."

"That sounds wonderful." He rubbed at his eyes and yawned.

"I'm sorry you didn't sleep. Was there something wrong with the room?" She felt lightheaded and so poured two glasses of orange juice, then placed one in front of Hawke.

"No. Honestly, it's perfect. I've been writing. The room seems to inspire me. I can't stop."

She tipped the coffee into his mug.

He poured some cream into it and took a sip. "By the way, you look lovely this morning."

"I, um, thank you." Sage took a quick look at her reflection in the microwave door and grimaced. The man had rocks in his head. She still wore pajamas, a flattering combination of Eric's bright orange SU T shirt and her faded, pink elephant long johns, and hadn't even brushed her hair. When she finally exhaled in one explosive sigh her hands shook and her knees trembled.

"Seriously, you look all tousled and much younger than the perfect hostess of Thistle Dew." He grinned.

"Thank you, I think."

He brought his coffee to his lips, smiling eyes looking at her over the rim of the mug, mouth curved in a smile. And so damned irresistible that Sage felt a longing to run gentle fingers through his hair as she walked by, just to make a connection. The instinctual female need to touch, to claim her man. Whoa! Where did that come from? Hawke wasn't her man. She didn't have time for such nonsense.

Sage fled the room to place the cream and sugar bowl on the buffet table in the dining room. Trembling a little, she shut the door in her mind on the previous thoughts.

She simply needed coffee.

She had to sit down.

All this over a silly little compliment? She chided herself. What am I doing? Why am I allowing this man to affect me this way? *Okay, Sage, calm down. He's a player. He's just toying with you. Control.* She took a deep cleansing breath. Ahhh. Much better.

Stoically composed, she returned to the kitchen determined to all but ignore Hawke. She worked efficiently, quietly, neatly tidying up her kitchen to a spotless shine after each task. She put warm muffins into a linen draped wicker basket, filled a bowl with fresh fruit and yogurt and then busied herself with several trips to the dining room with her offerings.

****

Hawke watched silently, sipping his coffee, enjoying the scenery and actually felt quite comfortable, quite at home. It surprised him, this feeling of belonging. Usually a sense of yearning plagued him, a subtle need to search for something. Here, at Thistle Dew he felt an odd, old-fashioned awareness of family. This was a sensation virtually foreign to him, but it brought back black and white flashes of his youth. Warm memories. Warm, despite the chilly aura Sage wore like a protective armor.

She looked soft this morning. He chuckled inwardly at the expression on her face when she realized she hadn't washed up or dressed yet. Her hair hung down in a single braid, escaping tendrils softening her face and her cheeks glowed with a natural rosy tint: a sharp contrast to her tired pale blue eyes.

Sage was a beautiful woman, Hawke concluded, although she didn't seem aware of it. He remembered her from the writer's weekend, a new widow, working frantically to build a business and ward off demons simultaneously. She hadn't mended completely yet, hell, it had been almost a year and Christmas must've been really difficult for her. He imagined her trying to maintain a festive atmosphere for Pia and any guests who chose to spend their holidays here. Of course she'd be too obstinate to close for the holidays.

Hawke had thought to spend the Christmas or New Year's Eve at Thistle Dew but there was literally 'no room at the Inn.' Since the writer's weekend in October, he couldn't stop thinking about her. Especially her eyes, smiling and friendly. Yet he could still see the aching sadness in their depths.

Since October he had returned to Thistle Dew only once, but unfortunately had very little opportunity to interact with Sage. Her overt avoidance of him did not further his self-confidence.

Outside the night gave way to the gray dawn, an owl hooted, and the chickadees gathered at the bird feeder near the window.

Pia came into the kitchen wearing pink princess pajamas, dragging a stuffed purple rabbit by the ears, and rubbing her sleepy eyes. She stopped. Her eyes swept the area for her mom and when she noticed Hawke smiling from his seat at the counter her eyes lit up.

"Hi, Mr. Hawke. Kristen said you came." She looked past him toward the swinging doors to the dining area. "Where's Mommy?"

At her silent request he reached down and lifted her on to the other counter stool. "She's getting things ready for breakfast." He watched the little girl yawn, and rub her upturned nose. Her mother's nose.

Then Pia gently sat her bunny on the counter and rested her head on its body. "Daddy used to make the breakfast."

Hawke felt a tug at his heart and wanted to hold her, hug her like he imagined her dad used to do; nuzzle his face into her sleep tousled curls. But recognizing the inappropriateness of that act and the misunderstanding of such an action, he simply asked, "How are you this morning, Little Princess?"

"Fine." She sat up and held up her rabbit. "This is Mr. Snuggles, but his secret name is Eric." She hugged the toy. "Don't tell Mommy though, 'cause she might cry."

"Okay, it'll be our secret." He brushed back a curl from her face.

"What will be your secret?" Sage entered the room and protectively lifted Pia into a morning hug. She swung Pia around and then plopped her on the floor. A quick turn and pat sent Pia towards their living space in the back.

Sage's dark glance back at Hawke warned him of a storm brewing.

"Mommy! You can't know people's secrets." Pia

54

giggled as they disappeared to wash up and dress.

Hawke refilled his coffee and waited. The fear reflected in her glance cut through him like a knife. Yet he understood her protectiveness. Sage, more than anyone, understood that a friendly gesture, a conversation or even a secret with a child could be suspected as something evil.

Loud talking in the dining room signaled that the rest of the guests were up and congregating. Familiar sounds of a buffet line indicated that by waiting for Sage to return, his muffin and fruit choices would be slim pickings. But he would wait and face her and Sage would realize that Hawke had nothing to hide.

A few minutes later, Sage stopped at the door and called back into their living quarters, "... then put your pajamas in the hamper." She had dressed for the day in a mid-length denim skirt and a pale blue turtleneck sweater. Her hair, still damp from a quick shower, had been re-braided and small silver hoops decorated her ears.

Without a glance in his direction she hurried to put on two padded oven mitts, pulled one pan from the oven, placed it on the stove top, then the other.

"My guests eat in the dining area, Mr. Hawke." Her tone, chilly before, now hung between them like icicles, as she carried the first pan of bubbling strata out to the buffet table.

He made no attempt to move, or speak. She clearly needed answers, but was determined not to show weakness or vulnerability. He needed to know what was going on.

There would be a confrontation, now better than later, in private better than public. He waited.

****

I have to admit Hawke, I'm impressed to see you still sitting there. She's not her best in the early morning hours; clumsy before coffee, not too good with conversation, and downright ornery if you press the right button.

Oh, Yes, and she packs a powerful verbal punch. You're about to find that out.

She's also very protective. Comes with being a mom, I guess. Over-protective even. An incident that happened when she was young made her overprotective. Maybe she'll tell you about it someday.

I watched you with my daughter. If I were sitting next to her on that stool, I would have held her on my lap, nuzzled my face in her curls and hugged her until the pain went away.

I can see you're a good man, Hawke. I'm just not convinced that my girls would be a priority in your famous author lifestyle. Will you always be there to keep them safe?

Having said that I'm not sure how I feel about having a stuffed purple rabbit named after me. It's very humbling.

Chapter 6

Hawke watched as Sage busily tended to the breakfast buffet. She seemed angry as she scurried between the kitchen and the dining area. He was determined to learn why she had been rude to him when he had only shown her and Pia friendship. He knew he was upsetting her by sitting in the kitchen as if he was welcome there. He decided to apologize.

Pia, dressed for the day, re-entered the kitchen. A glittering ribbon held tight a pony tail that had been brushed lovingly into one long curl. She wore a purple fleece hoodie that artistically advertised the Thistle Dew Bed and Breakfast. Her tiny jeans had purple flowers embroidered around the hem and down the outside seam of each leg. She walked with the air of a little princess who had plans for the day and meant to keep them.

Hawked grinned.

"Hi, Mr. Hawke." She climbed up onto the empty counter stool by herself. "After I eat my porridge, that's the same as oatmeal, but I like porridge 'cause the three bears eat it, I have to feed Pooh. He's always hungry in the morning." She shook her head with a comical air of maturity, then sprinkled a heaping teaspoonful of sugar over the waiting bowl of cereal and stirred. "What are your plans today, Mr. Hawke?"

"Well, I..." He paused to pass her a small pitcher of milk. She surprised him with her question.

The little girl concentrated on not spilling a drop, then set the pitcher down and continued. "Mommy says if people don't have plans they might waste their whole day and days are precious." Her smile made her eyes sparkle.

"I plan to go for a walk, maybe check out the pond, then write my story." He handed her a paper napkin. Having just thought it up, he figured his plan would pass muster. He tucked away the knowledge that Sage was teaching Pia to enjoy each day. Savoring his own time suddenly meant more because of a child's words. *Out of the mouths of babes.*

Pia considered his comment with a thoughtful expression. "I don't write stories yet, but I'm a really good colorer. I was thinking I should do some coloring today. My favorite things to color are flowers. Sometimes in winter we just need to see some beautiful flowers." She ate a spoonful of oatmeal. "Mommy bought me my own really big pad of paper, cause when I was little, I colored flowers on everything." She pointed to a small red flower decorating the bottom of the refrigerator. "Once I colored flowers on daddy's balls."

Hawke choked on a sip of coffee. He tried not to laugh out loud but swallowed a chuckle creeping up his throat.

"He wasn't even angry. He said they would bring him luck, but I don't think they did." She stopped eating and stared at the shelf where a putter and decorated golf ball were displayed.

Hawke remembered the first time he visited this kitchen and had seen the broken putter and the ball. He'd assumed the putter was the last one Eric ever used. And now he understood the significance of the ball. Eric's favorite. A tribute to a man long gone. A remembrance not forgotten. How could he compete with a ghost?

Whoa!

Where had that come from?

Hawke's thoughts were interrupted by Pia.

"That one with the blue flower was his favorite." Pia drank some orange juice. "You know what?"

"No." Hawke was grateful for her question. It stopped his wandering thoughts cold. "What?"

"I might take a walk today, too." She put a dripping spoonful into her mouth and swallowed. "Maybe we can walk together." She grinned as if it was decided. "Mr. Hawke?"

Uh oh, this sounded serious.

"Are you named after a bird?"

Hawke laughed, caught off-guard.

Sage smiled as she entered the kitchen.

"No. Not the bird." He noticed that he caught Sage's interest. He made eye contact to include her in the conversation.

She relaxed as she joined them at the counter.

"My mother said she named me for the King of Norway, King Haakon. But my father used to tease her and argue that she named me for her favorite box of chocolate called Kong Haakon. Either way, my name means I'm royalty and irresistible to women."

Sage rolled her eyes.

"What do you think, Pia?"

"I think you're like a king 'cause you're so big." Pia giggled as she touched his nose with her finger. "And your hair is the same color as chocolate." She hopped down from the stool and grinned. "You're like a bird too. Your eyes are like a hawk. Always watching. I gotta go feed Pooh. He's hungry." She went through the door of their private living area. Hawke could see she was standing at the coat rack climbing into her jacket and mittens.

"Whew, I guess she's got my number. Pretty perceptive kid."

"Yes, she is." Sage smiled softly. "Sometimes she really surprises me."

Pia returned to her mother's side with boots on the wrong feet, coat half buttoned and the lower legs of her snow pants unzipped.

Sage smiled and nodded at Pia's endless chatter as she helped her daughter fix her clothing, then placed a small plastic bowl of apple cores in her mittened hands and opened the back door.

"Hurry back, Sweet Pea."

"Okay Mommy." Pia carried the plastic bowl carefully down the porch steps singing "You Are My Sunshine" at the top of her lungs.

Sage stayed in the doorway watching her.

Hawke stood close behind, feeling the heat of her body warming his without touching.

"She's priceless." Hawke complimented as Sage closed the door.

"Yes she is, and thank you for saying so." She moved quickly to the dining room door. "I'm sorry. I don't have time for chit chat. I have to clear up after breakfast and start baking for tomorrow."

Hawke watched silently as she hurried out of the kitchen, grinned as she returned moments later with a stack of dishes and filled the dishwasher.

"So," Hawke began as he once again parked himself at the center island. "Is it all men, or just me?"

"About that," She looked out the window toward the barns, then continued placing glasses and mugs on the top rack. "I owe you an apology. It was uncalled for."

He remained silent, watching her bend over to put dirty silverware into the little cutlery boxes. The back pockets of her jeans sparkled with a heart shaped design. He thought it a perfect compliment to her heart shaped bottom.

"At first I thought you had an aversion to ALL men. But then I brilliantly rationalized that you had been married."

She left the room again and returned with more dishes.

He continued as if she'd never left. "And then during the writer's weekend, I watched as you conversed quite kindly with Andreas, Norman and even Dakota. Actually you've been amiable with most of the guests here, though you barely tolerate your handyman—but with me, you're well, cautious I guess would be a diplomatic way to put it." He paused and emptied his cup of cold coffee. "Are my books that bad?"

"I've only read a couple of your books. The Inn doesn't allow me much time to read."

After pressing the start button on the dishwasher, she sprayed the countertops with a disinfectant and scrubbed as if erasing inappropriate pictures from a school blackboard.

The pictures were inappropriate all right. The images that popped into his mind played like a spicy movie. But before there would be any spice, he would have to gently trace her jaw line with the back of his fingers to coax the anger away. Then he would ever so lightly trace his thumb over her lips to relax their straight line of irritation. Only then could he place a finger tip beneath her chin to gingerly encourage her to raise her eyes to meet his. And then he would silently relay the depth of his feelings. Only it wasn't his right. Not yet. Hawke sighed and mentally acknowledged he needed to take things slower and to earn her trust.

"She's afraid you'd cry if you knew that she renamed her purple bunny Eric."

"Pardon?"

"That's Pia's secret." He smiled. "I feel the need to have you trust me. I don't like telling her secret, but I hate you thinking the worst of me." He carried his mug to the sink. "I'm going for a walk. Would you like to join me?"

Sage hesitated. "Actually, I have to..."

"I promised to pick Pia up at the barn and check

out the pond with her."

Sage stared at him for long moments. Hawke waited patiently, thinking that if they moved this slow for every single thing he planned they'd be old as dirt before he'd ever get a chance to kiss her. Much less, anything else.

"Okay, I do need a break and I could use some fresh air." She offered a surrendering shrug as she tossed the dishcloth into an empty laundry basket and placed the spray cleaner back in its place under the sink. "I'll just get my jacket."

Maybe he'd get that kiss sooner than the next ice age.

Hawke had already done a quick check this morning on the internet and knew a forewarning of a winter storm was threatening the northeast. The frigid air suggested the storm was well on its way.

He waited just outside of the back door. He was enjoying the antics of the chickadees as they played at the birdfeeder. He turned at the sound of her opening the door.

Sage was bundled up for the harsh weather.

"Ready?"

"Yes. Let's get Pia." She descended the few steps to the shoveled walkway. She leaned against the rail and took a series of deep breaths.

"Are you all right?" Stepping quickly toward her he placed his gloved hand at her elbow for support.

"I was just dizzy for a second." She looked up at him and as their eyes met, he wetted his lips.

Hawke's hand slid down her arm slowly and he cautiously took her hand. They held hands as they headed toward the barn.

Lowell rounded the corner of the barn, his arms burdened with wood he had split for the fireplace when he saw them. Hawke thought that if looks could kill, Lowell's gaze would have fried him on the spot.

****

Ahhh, my little Sweet Pea. I heard you singing our song on your way out to the barn. You are my sunshine, Pia. I know you know I'm with you. When I make a cardinal sit on the fence and sing to you, you just say, 'Hi Daddy.'

You're getting to be such a big girl. I had plans to teach you how to ski this winter. I had plans to follow your school bus on your very first day of Kindergarten. I had plans to teach you how to dance. I had such great plans for us, Sweet Pea.

By the way, I can feel your warm hugs when you squeeze your purple bunny.

Chapter 7

The Inn was quiet. The cold weather encouraged an impromptu party at the pond. Children raced back to the Inn with a report of excellent skating conditions. The dads had gotten together to build a roaring bonfire and Mrs. Wilson brought a few bags of marshmallows. The kids broke off long sticks on their way through the woods and hurried back to the pond.

"I thought Thistle Dew was popular because of it's proximity to the ski slopes." Hawke pulled his collar up.

"We have the mountains for skiing in winter, hiking in summer, cross country skiing trails, and our own little pond for ice skating. A few of the families have been here before, an annual visit, and so they bring ice skates as well as skis."

They stopped at the barn to pick up Pia who was singing to Pooh as she fed him.

"Look at what I found." Pia proudly held a small white downy feather in the palm of her mitten.

"Sweet Pea, it's just a pigeon feather." Sage looked up into the rafters. "Put it down."

"It's Daddy's." Pia closed her hand around her prize. "He left it so I would know he's here."

Sage looked at Hawke when words escaped her.

Hawke knelt down to examine the feather more closely. "I'm no expert, but this is definitely not a pigeon feather." He reached into his pocket for the sales receipt from his coffee purchase and motioned for Pia to set the feather in the paper. Then he carefully folded the feather in the paper and placed it in his pocket.

"For safekeeping." He said to Pia, who nodded and reached for Hawke's hand.

The three walked along the short path that led to the pond, their breath making white puffs like old steam engines leaving for new horizons. Pia skipped along a few steps ahead of the adults.

"Look at me, Mr. Hawke!" Pia shouted as she fell backward into the pristine snow just on the edge of the path and proceeded to do a series of horizontal jumping jacks. Satisfied, she extended her hand, a silent plea for her mom to help her up. They all stepped back to admire her work. "That's my guardian angel." Pia proudly announced. "Her name is…umm….Snowflake."

"She's lovely." Sage complimented, then bent down to give Pia a hug. "You did a really good job."

"'member we made angels with Daddy?" Pia's blue eyes searched the depths of her mother's. Suddenly the memory of Daddy choked her and tears welled up.

Sage took Pia into her arms again.

Hawke stood silent for a minute and then felt inspired to lighten the moment with a comical antic.

"I think Snowflake is lonely." He said decisively. He placed his heels against the edge of the packed path and fell back with the aplomb of a tall tree. "Timber!"

White powdery snow poofed and he moved his arms and legs like an upside down frog swimming for shore. Pia giggled hysterically and Sage's laughter sounded like a trilling of the high notes on a piano.

With a little pleading from her daughter, Sage made a snow angel, too. She fell into a pillow of soft snow and windmilled her arms and legs. She stopped to stare into the heavens. Snowflakes melted on her face.

ALee Drake

"Did you fall asleep, Mommy?" Pia's concerned voice brought her back from her reverie.

With an audible sigh, Sage grounded herself.

She accepted Hawke's outstretched hand and the three silently regarded the family of snow angels. The littlest angel was protectively situated between the larger two angels.

In unspoken agreement they turned towards the pond.

From the edge of the woods, the pond was a scene from a Norman Rockwell painting, picture perfect, white and silent save for the intermittent giggles of children skating on the silver ice.

Nearby, seated on hand-hewn log benches, adults were watchful of the young skaters. The group immediately noticed Sage, Hawke and Pia. They waved.

"Can I go get my skates now?" Pia's excitement bubbled.

"Yes, they're in the shed."

Pia's double runners hung on a nail inside the door of a small red shed that sheltered firewood, blankets and extra mittens. Sage helped Pia strap them on over boots and took her to the ice.

A preteen girl in a cherry red skating outfit gracefully approached and extended her hand. Pia accepted and the two slipped, skated and fell their way around the ice.

"This is nice." Sage watched her child, smiling and periodically returning a wave. "Pia is really happy today."

"What about her mom?" Hawke watched the snowflakes melting on Sage's eyelashes and thought they made her eyes glisten with sweetness.

"I'm happy."

"Good." He looked into her eyes to read sincerity there. "You've got a lot on your plate. I'm impressed at how well you've balanced motherhood and

66

running Thistle Dew."

"Thanks. It was a struggle for a while." She was animated and even cheerful. "After Eric died no one thought that I could do it alone. Some even tried to talk me into giving it up."

She turned to watch Pia screeching with delight.

Hawke grinned as the little girl fell, bounced back up and did an awkward bend to remain upright.

"But you did."

"I was determined to make it work. I still am. I think Eric would be proud of me."

Sage had become strong. The Inn was flourishing and more than writers held conferences there now. Hawke knew because he'd been responsible for letting some of his friends know about the welcoming atmosphere and cozy ambiance of Thistle Dew.

"I'm sure of it." Hawke took a tenacious conversational step forward. "How did you two meet? Had you known each other long?"

"He saved my life."

"You've captured my interest."

"You really don't want to hear my life story." She smiled nervously.

"Actually, I do." He caught her gaze.

Sage took a few deep breaths.

Hawke could see by the expressions on her face that she was battling her decision. He waited patiently.

She blinked hard and then shook her head. "No big deal. He was just at the right place at the right time. That's all." She smiled nervously. "Lucky for me."

She didn't need to tell him.

He came across her terrifying story when he was doing the research for his book. The local news archives provided him with the whole sordid ordeal.

On microfiche he read a story of neighboring sixth grade students Sage and Lowell walking home from school one spring day, when a stranger forced Sage into his car.

The news story told of Lowell's futile attempt to attack the man and Sage trying to escape but the inside door handle had been removed. And then the man falling to the ground as a well-aimed baseball knocked him out, giving Eric the chance to pull Sage from the car. The man had been a pedophile, kidnapper and murderer wanted in a number of states.

It was this story that brought Hawke to Thistle Dew initially. The news story provided him with a valuable portrayal of an attempted kidnapping and rescue. He wanted to meet the survivor of that horrific experience. He wanted to know what kind of adult had emerged from the event. But since he met the woman, his interest in her story for his book research had waned. This woman had survived experiences that had crushed lesser people. Hawke was drawn to her like a moth to a flame. Her strength and spirit was so much more than the creased pages of an old newspaper story.

Hawke hoped that someday Sage would trust enough to tell him about it.

"Sage, come join us by the fire." One of the mothers called out. There were log benches outside the perimeter of the warm fire and Hawke led Sage over to a vacant space on one of the logs. Children were laughing and calling to parents, "Mom watch this." or "Dad did you see me go fast?"

"This is really lovely." One mother complimented.

"Thank you." Sage's eyes twinkled.

"Have you been in operation very long?" She asked as she clapped her mittens together at her son's antics on the ice.

"A few years." Sage watched Pia twirl, topple then throw her head back and laugh in complete delight.

"Our kids look forward to a weekend here every winter." Another mother added. "We have one day at the slopes and one day ice skating."

"My boys ski raced yesterday. It's nice to be able to relax afterwards." A man with a small boy snuggled on his lap spoke.

The little boy whispered to his dad.

"Oops, sorry. We're going to head back to the Inn. Bobby needs to use the rest room."

"Isn't that's the craziest thing? You spend a half hour getting them all bundled up against the cold and before they even get out the door they have to go to the bathroom."

There was a chorus of laughter.

"At least Bobby had some time to skate. I think he's also ready for a nap," his mother said.

"NO! Bobby tried to wriggle out of his father's arms. The man kissed his forehead, then proceeded to carry his crying son back through the patch of woods toward the Inn.

"I'd better help." The woman rose and called three young boys to come off the ice.

They obeyed but complained all the while.

"We're taking the boys to dinner at Chez Maurice to practice good manners." She explained.

"You're brave." Another mother chuckled. "We're going to Beefy Burgers. No dress code. No manners required."

"You'd be surprised at how well they step up to the plate

"Very interesting to watch parenting skills at work." Hawke leaned over and whispered to Sage.

"Or not." Sage nodded.

"We'd better get going too." One man signaled to his kids. "Before the roads get too bad."

The remaining couples at the fire gathered up their kids and belongings to head back to the Inn. The snow was coming down steadily now and the fire had been nearly extinguished.

Sage helped Pia remove her skates.

"Here, I'll hang them up for you."

Sage handed him the skates.

In the shed, Hawke easily found the rusty nail, then folded a blanket someone carelessly tossed over the wood pile. He caught a glimpse of white behind the door and reached down to retrieve a forgotten toy. Once outside he held up the toy.

"Does this little lady live in the shed?"

"Mommy! Look! It's Abigail." Pia grabbed the dirty doll. Abigail had been lost since Pia had been punished for spitting peas into her glass of milk last summer. She'd run away to hide in the shed beneath a blanket. Fortunately, Sage had seen Pia slip out the back door and had followed. She found her huddled in the shed crying at not being allowed to color for three days. Despite her pounding heart at her baby's escape, Sage calmly explained to Pia that she should always have a talk with Mommy when she was troubled.

"Oh Abigail I've missed you." Pia held her doll close.

Sage thanked Hawke with a grateful look.

"Eric gave Abigail to Pia when he returned from a business trip. We should head back to the house." She kissed Pia's forehead. "I'll bet Abigail would like a warm bath and some dry clothes."

"Okay Mommy. I think she would like some hot cocoa too."

"That's a good idea. When we get back, you can help me put together some snacks and hot chocolate for our guests."

"Oh, Abigail and I are good at helping, Mommy!"

They started on the path together until Pia

suggested they could walk faster if someone wanted to carry her.

When Sage automatically knelt, Hawke's placed his large hand on her shoulder.

"I'll carry her." He lifted Pia onto his broad shoulders and never said a word when she posed Abigail to sit like a princess on his head. "Whee! I'm almost as high as the sky!"

Hawke reached down for Sage's hand with confidence.

She looked up at her daughter and squeezed lightly.

"Thank you." She whispered shyly.

They walked peacefully as the snow gathered on the branches.

A few minutes later they paused at the corner of the barn. From there they could see the Inn. It looked breathtakingly dream-like as soft yellow light filtered through the windows. The smell of smoke wafted from the stone chimney.

"I want to show Kristen that I found Abigail." Pia wiggled, so Hawke was obliged to lower her to the path. "Elephant juice, Mommy." Then with a bundle of energy she scurried toward the house.

"Elephant juice?" Hawke's forehead wrinkled and his lips curved into a subtle grin.

"It's code for 'I love you'."

He waited for more explanation.

"If you mouth the words 'elephant juice' it looks like you're saying I love you."

When she demonstrated Hawke couldn't pry his gaze from her lips.

"Elephant juice to you, too." Hawke teased.

She gave him such a long look that he worried he'd spoken too soon. After a moment she reached out and brushed falling snow off his shoulders.

"It's been a perfect afternoon."

"Almost."

Hawke lifted his hand and took one of hers. He pulled one glove off and his warm fingers grazed her cheek as he gently tucked an itinerant tendril back under her knit hat. He smoothed his thumb over her lips, watching as she trembled in anticipation.

Their eyes locked together, each reading the others intentions, reaction, soul. He lowered his face, slowly, painstakingly slowly, giving her a chance to say no, allowing him to savor the sensations melting within him.

A snowflake landed on her upper lip and he impulsively licked it off. She shuddered but did not resist. Her breaths increased to little rapid puffs of warmth in the cold air.

He lowered his face, as close as he could without their lips touching. It was this moment, this moment of anticipation, heightened awareness and intense sensation that he wished to prolong, to make last forever.

But his mind warned him; the teasing had gone on long enough. "Taste her," it screamed, and he did. He touched.

Her lips quivered at first but warmed to him, soft and responding. Her arms reached around and pulled him closer. Their breaths mingled when he pulled away.

"My God." He whispered and he brought his head down for more.

He tested, brushing the tip of his tongue to her lips to see if he should venture further. Her mouth parted, welcoming him, and their flavors blended. The gentle stroking soon accelerated and, breathing ragged, both began to explore these fresh feelings with fervent fury.

The cold winter air and the blizzard blustering around them barely blew out the fires of their newfound passion. When they reluctantly separated, Sage laid her head on his chest.

Hawke rested his chin on her hair, arms holding her close.

"I don't think I should have..." She pushed hands against his chest. "We can't..."

"Shhhhhh. Our kiss was wonderful. I think we are both surprised at how amazing it was." He held on as she tried to wiggle away. "Sage. Look at me." He held her at arms length. It was hard to see in the white lacy air.

She looked into his eyes. Hers filled with tears.

"We both know that we share something powerful."

"I can't. I'm not ready." Her voice quivered.

Before Hawke could say anything a scolding flock of crows wildly burst into the air from the woods.

He gently caressed her face with his palms. "Then we'll take it slow."

He took her hand and they started toward the house.

Sage remained silent beside him, but he noticed she didn't remove her hand from his own.

As they were stomping the snow off their boots on the porch a pizza truck pulled into the only empty space in the small parking area. The teenager delivered his pizzas and apparently pleased with his tip, danced his way back to the small delivery truck.

Sage removed her coat and hung it on the coat rack. She turned, gave him a tentative smile, then headed to her kitchen. "I need to help Pia make snacks and hot drinks."

Hawke's smile curved as he anticipated hot cocoa, coffee and maybe some cookies. He walked into the great room just as the group gathered around the fireplace opened a pizza box. A persistent knock on the door could barely be heard above the commotion derived from serving pizza and soda. Hawke answered it since Sage had gone off to find

Pia.

"I found this in the snow in the parking lot. Somebody might be missing her." The teen held up a dirty, wet abandoned Abigail.

****

"Sage, quick, look!!!! Sage, watch Pia!! She's stopping by the parking lot. She's talking to someone in a car, showing her doll. Sage, what are you doing? Sage...

You're kissing him.

You're kissing him?

I knew you would at some point, knew he was the one to catch your eye, to catch your heart.

But Pia. Sage you will never forgive yourself if anything happens to Pia.

I will be with her. I will keep Pia safe for you.

And him. For both of you.

Chapter 8

So like kids, Hawke thought, a cherished doll one minute and forgotten toy the next. Something more exciting must have caught Pia's attention and Abigail was forgotten. Strange that her excitement over having found the doll hadn't even lasted as far as the house but then again, he didn't really know Pia. He turned toward the kitchen when Sage entered the great room with a puzzled expression.

"Kristen hasn't seen Pia, that little imp. I wonder where she is?" her eyes settled on the rumpled doll in Hawke's hands. "Oh good. You found Pia. Where is she?"

Hawke shook his head. "No, I haven't seen her."

"But you have Abigail?" her voice rose and her eyes darted to the adult guests. "Where did you find Abigail?"

"The pizza delivery boy found her in the parking lot." Hawke wished Pia would walk into the room so the look of fear crossing Sage's face would evaporate. When he saw the wave of panic flash in her eyes he handed her the doll. Hawke zipped his jacket and pulled the collar up. "I'll check the barn. She probably went back to check on Pooh."

Sage simply stared at the doll as if it could speak and tell her where Pia was. "We would have seen her go into the barn. I watched her until she reached the front walk. Then I...we... Oh...my...God."

Hawke could see the flow of her thoughts, the connections she was making to explain the moment she, they, took their watchful eyes off Pia. The kiss, it only lasted a minute, maybe less. It wasn't long enough...and yet it was too long. It was enough time for a little girl to disappear.

"Oh, my dear God." Sage whispered as she reached for a chair. She slowly lowered herself into it and pressed her fingers to her eyes.

He went to her, knelt beside her. "Sage." He whispered. He could only imagine where her thoughts were. Worst case scenarios. One particular scenario, one she had survived. Hawke could tell from her trembling body that she was revisiting the nightmare so many years ago.

"Sage, we'll keep looking until we find her."

Did she even hear him? The glazed look in her eyes let Hawke know she was lost in her memories, fighting the grip of a kidnapper.

"Pia? PIA!" She jumped up and ran back through the kitchen to their rooms. "Pia, where are you, Sweet Pea?"

The people in the dining room had stopped eating, some already placing napkins on the tables and half-rising from their chairs.

"Have any of you seen Pia? Do you know if she came into the house about ten or fifteen minutes ago?" Hawke asked.

"She was skating on the pond, last I saw her." One young man said. The others nodded in agreement.

"Okay, guys." One of the fathers stood up. "Get your stuff on, we need to go back outside."

"But Dad..." The ten year old pointed to his waiting slice of pizza.

"Now." The man ordered. "Let's find Pia."

"Would you guys mind going back to the pond?" Hawke asked as they bundled up in wet snow pants and soggy mittens.

The man nodded. Other guests were already crowding into the entry way, taking coats off hooks and slipping into mittens and boots.

Hawke went into the kitchen and returned a minute later with two flashlights and a whistle. He handed them to the boys. "Check the path through the woods, we made snow angels there. Remember to blow the whistle three times if you find her," he said. "And if you can't see because of the snow, blow five times so we can find you."

"We will, Mr. Hawke!"

"Let's stay together, boys." Mr. Hayes added. "We don't need to lose you in this weather too." He herded his boys out into the cold.

"Mr. Roberts," Hawke spoke to a man already dressed for the outside, "Could you check the parking area? All the cars inside and beneath. She might be hiding."

The man nodded, pulled his hat down and went out the door.

"Mrs. Hayes, could you and your girls check the guest rooms. I'll get you the master key." Hawke reached to a tray in a desk drawer. "Check every little cubbyhole you can find." He handed a ring of keys to the woman.

As he moved to close the drawer a bright color caught his eye. Hawke lifted the page neatly torn from a coloring book. It was the picture of a toy rabbit colored neatly with a purple crayon. *Purple bunny.*

He looked around the room. A purple bunny named Eric. Hawke shook his head. Next he'd be expecting to see Eric's ghost sitting on the mantle. Hawke looked down at the picture and felt a feathering 'something' brush against his mind. His body tingled with a sense of Pia's well-being. Was Pia's Daddy trying to tell him something? CRAZY!!!! Hawke quickly put the paper back into the drawer.

Struggling to hold his composure he turned to another woman dressed for outdoors and waiting for instructions.

"Mrs. Wilson, would you and Alexa mind searching the library upstairs?"

"Shouldn't we look outside?"

"I think we have enough searchers out there."

Both slipped out of their coats and hurried up the steps.

Andreas and Dakota entered the great room, brushing snow off their jackets and pulling gloves off to hang on the mitten-drying rack Sage had placed next to the coat pegs.

"What's all the commotion?" Dakota asked.

"Sage's daughter, Pia, is missing." Hawke opened the door.

"What do you want us to do?" Dakota was all business, already putting his jacket and gloves back on.

"Could you check if she's in the cellar?"

"Will do." The men went back out into the cold.

Hawke quickly headed to the barn. He recited a mantra of prayer. *Please let her be with Pooh.* The last time he prayed he was fourteen years old. At that time he asked God to help his Dad to get better. His prayer went unanswered. The next few weeks became a blur of nightmares; a botched surgery and funeral arrangements. The months that followed were one continuous nightmare as his mother struggled to pay the rent and buy the medicine necessary to keep her son alive.

Hawke didn't want Sage to experience that kind of terror ever again. She'd already lost her husband. Could she bear the loss of a child, too? Hawke stopped the thoughts. His heart clenched as he remembered Pia's delighted laughter over the snow angels. *If there's a guardian angel for this child, please protect her. Please bring her back to her mother. Please let me see that little girl's smile and know that I made her happy. Please don't let me lose her.* Hawke felt his soul stutter. *When had she climbed into his heart?* He was astounded at the sense of loss that made him ache. Pia was just a baby. His sweet little girl, whom he cherished. Somehow, that laughing child had crept into his life, sparking a warm glow he'd not felt in years. His prayers intensified as he opened the great door.

The barn was quiet. The soft murmurings of the alpacas, the muffled meows of cat conversations and the whistle of wind trying to sneak into the barn were the only sounds.

"Pia." He called repeatedly as he carefully checked each stall then climbed into the hay loft. "Pia. Where are you?"

Hope choked in his chest. He had to find Pia. On his way back to the house he walked around the parking area and front porch but the snow and wind had already erased any hint of a child's footprints. Hawke reentered the house to hear Sage still frantically calling Pia's name.

"Maribelle, would you please call 911?" We need help. The blizzard is getting worse," Hawke said as he neared the check-in counter.

"I thought for sure you'd find her in the barn." Maribelle reached for her cell phone and dialed.

"No, and the snow has already covered up the sidewalks."

Mr. Roberts returned and quietly reported his findings. Hawke felt his soul clench. "I'll walk the length of the driveway. "Maribelle, would you stay by phone? Thanks." He rushed back into the storm. "Mr. Roberts, walk with me. We can cover twice as much area together."

"She may have fallen into a ditch." Mr. Roberts suggested. Hawke nodded as the two walked out into the snowy landscape.

What began as a lovely evening snowfall suddenly became a blustery blinding blizzard.

Visibility was hampered by huge white snowflakes being blown in big circles by a frigid north wind.

Less than a half hour later Sage's police friend, Peter, and his deputy, Danny, arrived in a patrol car. They began to interview the guests.

Men from the local volunteer fire department proceeded with their systematic search and rescue tactics in and around Thistle Dew in a mass effort to find the missing child.

As the Hayes family, the Wilsons, Mr. Roberts and Hawke returned looking like shivering snowmen, Peter asked everyone to gather in the great room.

Hawke watched as Sage kept busy brewing coffee and serving the kids hot chocolate from a huge cauldron she had simmering on the soup and salad bar sideboard.

Peter asked questions of the group while Danny took notes.

"So, she was last seen ice skating at the pond." Peter reiterated his findings. "And she was with her mother and Hawke. Is that right?"

Heads nodded.

Peter turned to Hawke, who sat at the edge of a straight back chair rubbing warmth back into his hands. "You left the pond area with Pia, then?" Peter asked. "Then you know she isn't at the pond."

"Yes." Hawke nodded. "She came with us. I carried her on my shoulders."

"Good." Peter looked at Sage. "I need to top off my coffee." Let's go into the kitchen. Sage. Mr. Hawke."

The three walked through the kitchen doors. Sage filled Peter's mug and sat on a counter stool opposite Hawke.

"You carried her on your shoulders." Peter repeated to Hawke. "Then what?"

"She wanted to run to the house to show Kristen

her doll," Sage explained.

"Did you see her run to the house?"

Sage shook her head. Tears filled her eyes.

"No," Hawke admitted. "We watched her go part way."

"Where were you?"

"We stopped by the barn." Sage seemed to study her trembling hands.

"Okay. I know you can see the house from the barn."

"She ran up the sidewalk toward the house." Hawke offered.

"Had she passed the parking area when you last saw her?"

"No. Not quite." Sage looked at Hawke with accusation.

"Then how is it that both of you saw her go past the barn, but didn't notice when she made it past the parking lot?" Pete was like a dog with a bone, tugging answers from them.

"We...ah...stopped at the barn." Hawke said.

"Why?" Pete was relentless.

"We...ahhh...were talking." Hawke felt his face warm and wondered when he'd ever blushed over anything after his teen years.

"I see." Pete's face was completely impassive.

"But the parking lot is where the pizza delivery boy found Pia's doll." Sage voice quivered.

"Okay. I'm sending out an Amber Alert right now." Peter took out his phone and made a call.

"Where could she be?" Sage wept.

Peter held her.

Hawke felt helpless.

"Excuse me," Maribelle interrupted as she poked her head in the door. "Is your handyman still here? The knob came off one of the dresser drawers."

Peter looked at Sage. "What time did Lowell leave this afternoon?"

Chapter 9

Hawke watched as the police chief placed a hushed call on his cell-phone. He figured the officer was discreetly ascertaining Lowell's whereabouts.

They had moved to the lounge area in Sage's office.

"You okay?" He turned to see if Sage was aware of the drama involving her handyman.

"I can't get warm." Sage shivered uncontrollably.

Hawke took an afghan from a chair by the fireplace and draped it around her. He dropped an arm across her shoulders offering strength. A knot formed in his stomach and his knees went weak. He didn't feel strong.

"Let's sit down."

Although he had been a sickly child, a weak adolescent and a scrawny young adult, he had been emotionally firm with most challenges. Sweet little Pia, who was missing and who'd somehow snuck into his heart while his back was turned, was tearing him to pieces. It surprised him that his heart hurt, like a migraine, with worry. *Is this what it feels like to care? When you feel like your core has been exposed and worms are feasting?* Slow pain.

My Glory, and if it is this agonizing for me, He looked down at Sage's trembling form, *I can not even imagine what she is going through.* He hugged her close. He had no comforting words to offer. He hoped she found some reassurance in his ministrations.

Through the open doorway Hawke watched as one of the search teams returned, blowing into the house with gusts of snow. They stomped their feet and headed to the stone fireplace in the great room to thaw.

"There's coffee, hot chocolate and a vat of chicken soup on the sideboard, guys." Peter announced through the open doorway of Sage's office.

Sage seemed unaware of the sudden chaos.

Hawke approached one of the rescuers. "Did you have any luck?"

The man lowered his eyes and shook his head. "No. Nothing."

"Where could she be?" Hawke whispered. He crossed the room to stand by the window. "Where are you, little Pia?" He felt the sting of tears. "Please be safe." Images, like nightmares, of Pia crouched in the snow, her cries muffled by the icy wind, plagued him. "Eric, please keep her safe." His warm breath fogged the icy window pane.

He heard Sage sniff and returned to kneel by her chair. She rested her head against his shoulder and he touched his lips gently to her crown.

The police chief studied the crowd out in the great room as if assimilating the scene. He paused, nodded to Hawke, then answered his cell phone. Peter then turned his back to Hawke and Sage and responded to the caller in a subdued tone.

Hawke strained to listen to the chief's conversation, but to shift his position might disturb Sage as she snuggled up against him.

"My sweet Sage," He whispered so softly it was more like a gentle breath. As he held her, he knew then, without a doubt, that he wanted Sage and Pia as his very own. *Forever.*

He loved them.

Peter walked over and knelt in front Sage.

She looked at him, asking without words.

"Lowell is at home." We're questioning him as to when he last saw Pia and if he knows where she might have gone."

"Lowell left hours ago, Peter." Sage stared at her friend, brows knit. "What are you suggesting?" She looked at Peter, suddenly realizing that Lowell was suspect. As she stood, the afghan pooled on the floor. "No. He genuinely cares for her. He has her around whenever he's here. Why? Why would he take her?" Sage shook her head and wrung her hands. "No. It's not Lowell. It just doesn't make sense. We lived next door to each other. We were best friends. Like brother and sister."

"That may be how it was for you, Sage, but I happen to know he was convinced that you belonged to him," Danny said. "He threatened all the boys in Mrs. Field's room to stay away from you. Told us in third grade how he was going to marry you."

"He did?" Sage was dumbfounded. "But that's just kid stuff." She sat back down, breathing as if she had just run a mile. "What does it have to do with finding Pia?"

"The day Eric saved you, Lowell climbed the hanging tree in Knott's Cemetery and cried."

"Why?" Hawke asked intrigued.

"Because the new kid in school, Eric, beaned Link and saved Sage. He hated Eric for that."

"What?" Sage was appalled. "He didn't hate Eric. They were best friends. Best friends up until the day Eric died. You must be mistaken. Lowell stood up for Eric at our wedding. It doesn't make sense."

"Lowell would do anything to be a part of your life. That's what he told me at your reception."

"I may be hearing possible motive." Peter interjected. "Jealousy. He may think that Pia should rightfully be his."

"Or maybe," Danny offered, "Lowell wants to be the hero this time, so he's hidden Pia away and will rescue her and you will be forever indebted to him."

"That's crazy." Sage dismissed their theories. "Lowell wouldn't hurt me like that. Or Pia. No. It's not Lowell."

Hawke could feel the tension building between the three of them. Sage was stiff with resentment, shrugging off his arm to glare at Peter. Sensing a confrontation between the friends, he quietly left the room so they could have their argument in private.

Kristin waved to him from the desk. She handed him a sheaf of papers.

"Could you take these in to the chief?"

He nodded, not wanting to step back into the room where he could hear Danny's voice rise sharply. They silenced as he came back in. Small town loyalty at its best. Sage's friends were protecting her even now. Danny eyed him and then walked into the kitchen.

Hawke waved the computer printout. "I don't mean to intrude, but here are the guest registers you requested. Kristen asked me to bring this in to you since she's busy helping one of the guests." He crossed the room in easy strides and offered the papers to the police chief.

Peter quickly shuffled through the sheaf of papers and handed them to Sage. "See if any one who has stayed here has given you cause to mistrust them."

"What? Why?"

Danny returned with two mugs of coffee, one of which he handed to his boss.

Peter took a sip of his coffee, as if he wanted to delay his answer.

Sage looked up at him.

"It could be someone who stayed here, Sage. Stayed specifically to target Pia."

Hawke had never seen someone's face turn bloodless white. Sage's eyes were huge, haunted pools.

He put a hand on her shoulder, feeling a vast relief when she reached up and squeezed. Her hands felt as cold as ice. Her grip tightened, and he didn't flinch from the lifeline she sought.

In the silence, Hawke knew he had to offer what he could. "Peter, have you had much experience with this type of situation?"

"I say this with both thanks and now regret, that no, I haven't ever experienced a child abduction. This is a small, quiet town. The most I have to worry about are speeders and marijuana parties under the bleachers at the high school."

"My book concerns the abduction of a child."

"That's right," Sage remembered. "You talked about it at the writer's weekend."

Sage seemed to be focused on the snowflakes accumulating on a pane of glass across the room.

He continued speaking to the men. "I've researched this in detail. The investigation is methodical. Sage, that's why it's imperative that you go through the guest lists. We need to call each person if necessary. Before Pia's disappearance hits the news."

Now that he had the undivided attention of all three he finished, "Let's face it, a number of people have had the opportunity to meet Pia." He sat in a chair across from Sage, "Has anyone shown an inappropriate interest in her, or been outwardly affectionate with her?"

"No! Never!" Fear returned to her eyes, sharpened the blueness, but tears blurred her vision. "What are you suggesting?"

"Continue, Mr. Hawke." Peter showed a keen interest.

"Hawke. Just Hawke." He spoke directly to Sage, "Listen Sage. Pia is a precious little girl. And beautiful."

Sage smiled weakly.

Peter was watching Hawke...like a hawk. Hawke found no pleasure in the word play.

"Maybe you noticed a childless couple who stayed here making a fuss over Pia? Or a man or woman who made a comment like they wished Pia was their child?"

Sage shook her head. "No. Yes." She reached for the papers. "Yes, there might be a clue here. Let me look at the lists."

"Every registered guest is listed here and you can see the number of guests that have returned, twice, three times and look." Hawke pointed to a series of lines highlighted in red. "Mr. Reginald Stockman has been here six times this year."

"He's a salesman. We're on his route."

"Think, Sage. Read each name carefully."

Sage studied the list.

The men waited silently.

She paused to look at them. "Please. I can't concentrate with the three of you watching me. There's plenty to eat in the kitchen and snacks on the sideboard."

Peter flashed a signal to his deputy and Hawke. Reluctantly, the men took the hint and left the room.

Hawke returned a few minutes later with a spinach and cheese omelet and a cup of coffee. He placed them on the table near Sage.

"Thank you." She barely glanced up from the list.

Slowly she began to nibble at the omelet while checking off some names, circling others.

Peter asked questions about each guest as she worked. He wrote in his notebook and a few times stepped away to place a discreet phone call.

Hawke watched her work for a few minutes, and then slipped quietly out of the room to check on the searchers coming in and out.

The news was not good. Weary men and women

thawed out by the fireplace and took mugs and snacks from Sage's guests, who were helping to keep them supplied. As soon as the people finished, they suited up and went back out into the blizzard.

Hawke returned to the office.

Sage looked up at him with tears and sniffles. "These people. They've become friends, some even like family. I can't find anyone really who I am concerned about. They were friendly to Pia and me and to each other. That is the atmosphere I have worked to create for this Inn. It's warm and friendly."

Hawke sat next to her and took her hand, "Yes it is." He shifted to meet her gaze. "But, someone has overstepped his or her bounds. Someone took warm and friendly and made it cold and dangerous. If you're sure it's not someone on this guest list, then where do we go next? Preschool? Church?"

Sage shook her head.

"What if it's a stranger?" Danny asked as he came into the room.

"I don't think so." Hawke returned, "This place is too far out of the way for a passer-by to just happen to pull into the parking area, see a little girl and take her."

"It seems far fetched, but sadly it has happened that way. We can't rule out any situation." Peter admonished. "Out of the way is what some..." He broke off, looking at Sage. "It's what some people look for." He finished, his expression tight.

Sage didn't seem to realize she was clinging to Hawke's hand again.

He kept still, feeling her icy fingers warm to his touch.

"I know it's not impossible, but honestly I don't think Pia would willingly go in a car with a stranger. Do you, Sage?" Hawke asked, to break her concentration on whatever horror had her gripping his hand with such intensity.

"Definitely not." Sage seemed encouraged. "We discussed that many, many times. Stranger danger."

"The only problem is that here, in this environment, people come as strangers and leave as friends." Hawke reasoned.

"So where does that leave us?" Peter pressed on his temples as if trying to discourage a brewing headache. He paced from door to window, left the room for a minute then continued his stroll, stopping only momentarily to touch a photo of Eric, Sage and Pia by the pond.

"It leaves us to assume that Pia is with someone she trusts. Someone who will not hurt her. Someone who will take good care of her." Hawke surmised.

Sage's shoulders relaxed and the worry in her eyes lightened up, just a little.

"And who will, at some point, bring her home." Danny contributed.

"But why would someone who cares take her in the first place?" Sage questioned the group. "That is something I cannot, for the life of me, understand."

"Me, neither." Peter sat on the sofa, stood, and then continued pacing.

"Does she know your phone number?" Danny asked.

"Yes." Sage whispered.

"Then she may call."

"Oh God. I hope so."

"Well, it's nearly midnight. She's probably asleep. She might not even know she's been taken without your approval."

"I don't know if I can take it. It's too much. First Eric. Then Pia." Sage broke down.

Peter came close and crouched down in front of her chair, holding out his hands. Sage reached for them, holding tight.

Hawke felt bereft, losing the warmth of her

fingers in his own palms.

"I wish I had the answers you need to ease your pain."

Peter soothed. "You're a strong girl, that's for sure. After Eric's death most of the town's people figured you'd give up Thistle Dew. But you held it all together." He reached up and squeezed her shoulders. "I have a team of good men, Sage. Smart, reliable. They will search non-stop until we find Pia."

"Why don't you lie down, Sage? I know you won't sleep but you will need to be refreshed in the morning." Danny tried to ease her pain.

"No. I can't." She sniffed. "I should be doing something. I should be looking."

Danny handed her the box of tissues from the end table.

"There are a lot of people looking for her. She will need to see you awake and happy when she comes home."

"I need to be doing something. I'll make some muffins or something." Sage leaned forward as if to rise. "I don't have the energy." She burst into tears.

Peter pressed her back into the chair. "You don't have to sleep. Just rest a minute. I need to go take care of some things. You stay here."

"I should..." Sage's voice tapered off.

"I'll stay with her." Hawke volunteered, reading Peter's need for discretion correctly.

"You're right. She shouldn't be alone. I'll get Ruthie in here."

Hawke heard the faint suspicion in Peter's tone, and made eye contact, trying his best to calm any worries Peter had. Pete's glance acknowledged him without expression.

"Ruthie's here?" Sage asked, her eyes lighting despite her anxiety.

"Yep." Pete broke Hawk's gaze to look at Sage.

"She's been helping Kristin handle the guests and the searchers."

"Oh, thank you. Thank her..." Sage murmured, trailing off as Peter walked over to the doorway.

"Ruthie." He called softly into the great room where a crowd kept vigil.

Hawke noted that people were mostly silent, speaking in hushed tones to the searchers moving in and out. A group of writers, guests and Sage's friends retreated to one of the conversation areas to wait for the next crowd of wet, cold professionals to come in.

Ruthie hurried to the doorway between the rooms. She listened to her husband's quiet instructions, nodded and after Peter touched his lips to her forehead, she came into the office.

Ruthie led Sage over to a more comfortable chair near one of the windows, its panes covered in snowdrift and delicate flakes as the blizzard swirled outside.

Hawke stood up and went to the open doorway, checking every corner of the great room in a vain attempt to see if Pia was hiding under a table or behind the sideboard. As if she'd pop out of the cupboards beneath. He sighed mentally. If only it were that simple. He glanced down at the carpet and saw the glittering chain. He bent and picked it up. The only woman in and out of the room in the past few minutes was Ruthie.

"Ruth, did you drop your bracelet?" He held up the short silver chain with three small stones and one large crystal.

"Oh, thank you. Where did I drop this?" Ruthie took the chain by the small silver bead at one end and let the crystal hang like an ornament from her fingers. "This is my pendulum."

Hawke watched as Ruth placed her flat left hand about two inches beneath the crystal.

Sage leaned weakly against some pillows, watching Ruth with little interest.

"Eric, if you are here today," Ruth spoke quietly, "please show me a yes."

Hawke felt his eyebrows climb into his hairline. What was this? Calling forth ghosts to find Pia? He noticed that neither Danny nor Pete seemed surprised and in fact, they went about their whispered consultation without acknowledging the women at all. Hawke watched in fascinated silence.

The pendulum moved slowly above the length of Ruth's outstretched hand.

"And show me a no."

The crystal slowed, circled then moved across her palm from the base of her index finger to the base of her pinky.

"Put it away, Ruth." Sage mumbled, "You know that stuff is mumbo-jumbo."

Ruth ignored her. "Eric, do you know where Pia is?" The pendulum slowed then vigorously swung from her wrist to her fingertips. "Is Pia all right?"

The pendulum continued swinging the length of Ruth's hand.

"She's ok."

"Ruth, put it away. It was already swinging when you asked it. It's just a joke. Put it away. You're so sweet Ruth, but I don't believe a swinging crystal can tell me anything."

"Eric, is Pia in danger?" They watched as the pendulum slowly changed its course. "Sage, Eric says Pia is not in danger."

"Put it away!" Sage started crying. "Please Ruth, Eric can't tell you how Pia is. Eric's dead. And Pia is..." She shook with uncontrollable sobbing.

Ruth dropped the crystal on the table, jumped from her chair and reached in to gather Sage into a hug.

Peter finished his conversation into his cell-phone, gave Hawke a hard stare and then raised an inquiring brow and motioned for Danny and Hawke to accompany him.

The men left the room, and Peter sat at the kitchen counter, directing his men, making notes and poring over the guest list that Sage had marked up.

Hawke felt useless, but when he made to leave, Peter motioned him to stay.

"Might need more advice." His terse comment made Hawke think that Peter hadn't moved him off the suspect list yet. Despite the fact that Sage was his alibi.

Throughout the night, people moved in and out of Thistle Dew in hushed silence.

Ruthie came in and took a cup of coffee.

Peter raised a questioning eyebrow.

"She's looking out the window and every once in a while her eyes shut for a time...she drifts off and then snaps awake. Just keeps staring out that window. But she's getting a little rest, despite her worry."

Ruthie left as quietly as she'd come in, not waiting for a response from her husband or Hawke.

Morning dawned somber, with the pall of fear for the child who might be lost in the snow.

Peter had sent some of his men home to rest, asking them to return in shifts.

The guests had arranged some sort of schedule, too, Hawke noted, with the women putting the kids to bed, then returning to help keep the searchers supplied. The male guests had arranged to go out with different parties, since they, too, knew Pia on sight.

Dawn's streaky sunlit fingers were peeking through storm clouds when more search and rescue teams showed up from a nearby town. Peter went to the group, leaving Hawke at the kitchen table with

Danny.

Kristen came in on a gust of snowy ice as the door banged open in the great room.

She peeked into the kitchen. "Good morning." she whispered. "I just wanted you to know that I'm here. How is Sage?"

"She's with Ruthie in the office lounge. She dozed a little from what Ruthie says."

Kristen nodded. "I'd better get something started for the guests' breakfasts." She peeked into the large refrigerator. "They'll be coming down soon. Sage will not want them to get anything but the best."

"Under the circumstances, "Hawke began, "I would hope they could survive on their own for the day. There are restaurants in town they could visit."

"In this storm?" Sage entered the kitchen, her single braid showed the only signs of a fretful night. "I'll make them breakfast." She took fresh fruit out of the refrigerator. "I'll need to keep busy until Pia comes home." She spoke calmly, confidently. "She'll be home today."

The men and Kristen stared at her momentarily, eyes silently speaking to each other; Is she all right? Did she hear something?

Peter went into Sage's office for a couple minutes. He returned to the kitchen and drank from the fresh mug of coffee Sage put in front of him.

"Ruthie's asleep."

"Yes, I told her to curl up and catch a few winks while I made breakfast."

Kristen gave Sage a strange look, took her mug and a plate of fruits and cheeses she'd scrounged and left the room without a word.

"I know you might think this is crazy, but the strangest thing happened during the night." Sage set about putting together a fruit salad, talking as she moved around the kitchen, "I remember crying, maybe just whimpering, and I was praying. To God, Jesus, Eric, anybody who would listen really. Just give me a sign, I asked, a sign that she's all right."

The group waited silently, no one dared to move, all spellbound by Sage's dream.

"And then I felt warm, a warmth like a hug." She wrapped arms around herself and inhaled deeply. Her eyes closed and her head tilted up. "And I smelled Eric's scent, fresh air, mowed grass, alpaca and a touch of car engine. I didn't exactly hear the words, but Eric told me that Pia is safe and she'll be home soon." Sage opened her eyes and smiled. "Anyone for hot coffee?"

The room was silent for a few minutes until Danny asked, "Did Eric tell you where she is or who has her?"

Sage moved to the stove where Kristen had laid out the ingredients for French toast. "Well, no." She began to mix eggs in a bowl. "But I sort of saw her." She dipped slices of bread into the egg mixture and placed the pieces evenly on the hot griddle. "Pia was sleeping under a blanket- warm, contented, safe."

"What else did you see? A room? A vehicle? The face of someone holding her or pulling the blanket up over her shoulders?"

Sage's mouth opened slightly and she looked above her kitchen window with concentration.

Hawke felt a shiver of something...he could see that the blizzard had stopped and the snow lay crisp and untouched on the ground. Bright sunshine made it almost painful to look out. And then he heard it.

The chimes shivered just above the window, untouched by any passing draft. A few strands of Sage's hair fluttered and then it was gone.

Hawke replayed the scene in his mind. He looked up at the ceiling, down at the floor and saw no vents, or grills to indicate that a furnace had gone on and the lift of air had caused that faint breeze inside the kitchen. There was nothing.

No one else seemed to notice.

But Sage had relaxed even more, her smile bright, her expression filled with hope.

"Please God, bring her little girl back." His silent prayer lifted to heaven on the faint trill of the chimes.

****

Eric sat on the counter smiling. He painted a dream for Sage and she not only remembered it, she believed it. She looked very tired, understandably stressed. He hadn't seen her look so drawn and pale since his funeral.

I'm communicating to you the best I can. It's good that you see and believe the dreams I send to you. I could tell you more to ease your anxiety. I could let you know that I am with her and she is safe.

How can I get Ruthie to remember to use her crystal pendulum? If only Ruthie would ask questions of her pendulum.

Yes, Ruthie use your crystal. My energy can direct the pendulum's direction. Please believe it, Sage. I never believed it either when Ruthie would take out her crystal. I thought she was making it move. But I know better now. For now I will continue to try to let you know I am with you. He reached out to touch her soft hair, but touching was not one of his capabilities. He blew on her hair instead, watched in satisfaction as a few loose strands danced in his breath and the chimes above her head tinkled in the breeze.

Chapter 10

Sage heaped the French toast into the warming pans and then started a huge batch of scrambled eggs.

She gave Pete, Hawke and Danny a pointed look.

"If you guys could go hold your pow-wow in my office I'd appreciate it. I have people to feed."

Pete and Danny immediately claimed the office desk, leaving Hawke to hover by the doorway, watching the people milling around in the great room and shifting so he could see into the kitchen, too.

Kristin had propped the swinging door open so the searchers could easily go in and out for hot coffee and food.

Sage invited the women guests who'd manned her kitchen the night before in once again and fed them first.

"Mrs. Hayes, Mrs. Wilson, I cannot thank you enough for helping me." She filled orange juice glasses and passed them to the two ladies at the counter. Both women looked exhausted. They had stayed up all night keeping the food and drinks going to the SAR teams.

"It was the least we could do." Mrs. Hayes patted Sage's nearest hand.

"Well, you two need to go rest after you finish your meal." She smiled. "I'll have Kristen keep the kids occupied down here."

The ladies ate quickly and went upstairs.

Sage and Kristin loaded up the soup and salad

sideboard with fluffy scrambled eggs, hash browns, pancakes and other goodies. Breakfast in the great room was filled with people.

The teams reported to Peter where they had searched and where they would be searching next. Then they moved to gobble down food and drink before heading back out.

Pete had called a dog team from the next town and asked Sage for an article of Pia's clothing.

Without a word, Sage handed him a shoe that was inside the door of their living quarters.

Sage went to the group of writers who were eating at one end of the great room.

"I want you all to continue your conference workshops. I know you are on limited schedules and you need to finish your work. I also know that you have a deadline for those contest entries. The professionals are out there looking, so I think they can spare you now."

She noted that despite their concern, there were looks of relief, too. She offered the lounge area of her office so they could work without interrupting the flow of SAR teams who were now using her great room as a staging area. Pete moved his base of operations out to the dining area.

The writers moved to her lounge.

Sage took a moment to think about how the Inn had transitioned easily with two completely different groups using the facilities. With some extra help once Pia was in school, she could start doing more than just the writer's conferences. Her thoughts broke off. Only after Pia was safe. Eric had promised. She just knew he would keep his little girl from harm.

Sage returned to her kitchen to find Hawke at the counter, talking to Peter.

"Hawke, the writers are continuing the conference and will probably want you to be present.

I think they are working on that contest thing someone told me about." She waved vaguely as she went to the sink.

Peter nodded to Hawke. "Go ahead, man. We've got the pros here and if I need you, I'll interrupt, if that's all right."

"I'd rather..."

"Hawke, the more normal things are, the better it will be when Pia returns. I don't want the writers upset enough to never come back. Please, go about the normal routine."

Sage was so entreating that he caved in.

He entered the lounge to find a minor mystery.

"Where IS Norman by the way? He isn't ill is he?" Dakota looked up as Hawke entered.

"Norman usually let's us know if he can't make it. And with this storm...should we call him?" Andreas was concerned.

"We've got the whole damn police force sitting downstairs drinking coffee. Don't you think they might have mentioned it if Norman had been involved in a car accident?" Maribelle was cranky.

Hawke wondered if she'd gotten any sleep last night. She'd manned the desk and the phones the night before, taking to receptionist duties like a pro.

Dakota left the room to check if Norman had made contact with Thistle Dew. He returned within minutes.

"Apparently Norman called Kristen yesterday to say he couldn't make it this weekend."

"Is he sick?" Andreas asked.

"I think it's about his wife. He told Kristen he needed to be with her."

"Okay, that's good to know. At least we know he's not in a ditch somewhere in this storm." Hawke was relieved.

"Let's get down to business."

The winter storm raged on. The police manned

the roadblocks and took turns dropping by the Inn to warm up and be fed. Searchers fanned out, going further and further a field.

No one had seen Pia. The little girl had been missing for nearly twenty—four hours.

Sage cooked and baked all day.

Hawke kept an eye on her, dropping in to get more coffee, cookies, or simply help carry trays of food out to the great room.

The sanguinity with which she woke slowly diminished like the cookies and warm breads she brought to the table. Except for the SAR teams, no one wanted a meal, but people nibbled all day.

Sage refilled mugs, brought out more food and with Kristen's help, kept the authors in the lounge well-supplied as they worked through their materials.

Peter and Danny, called to the scene of a multiple car accident, were gone for hours.

Hawke divided his time between the writer's workshop, the kitchen and his room. He spent time on the internet and his cell phone. He searched every avenue, touched base with every resource he knew. And came up frustratingly empty. He went downstairs to the kitchen where he found Sage alone, scrubbing the counter tops with enough force to wipe off the color.

"How are you doing?" He wanted to hold her, to offer comfort, but with all the people around he wasn't sure if she'd accept it.

"Fine." She continued spraying and polishing the counters. "Please go."

"She'll be okay."

"I know."

"We'll find her."

"Peter will." She looked him in the eye. "I would like you to leave my kitchen, please."

"You're angry at me. Why?"

"No. Not angry."

"Then what?"

"Angry at me." Her voice began to quiver. "I should have walked with her to the house. She wouldn't be missing if I had walked with her to the house."

"We took our eyes off her for a second."

"Exactly. And it was a second too long wasn't it?"

"My God, Sage, it was just a simple kiss." Hawke instantly regretted the callousness of that comment when he noticed the rage creep into her eyes, then immediately evaporate into genuine pain.

"It was not just a kiss, Hawke." She turned to face him, "It was my first kiss. My first kiss since Eric. And it was not simple. To me. A kiss is not simple if it made me feel so warm that when it was over I was surprised that it was still snowing. My mind celebrated the sensations of that kiss with such an explosion of colors the dusk momentarily blinded me." She buried her face in her palms, pressed her fingertips in her eyes, and sighed heavily. "I think that my antipathy could be directly related to the fact that those few stolen moments have altered my life forever. And to you it was just a simple kiss."

Hawke only heard her confession hidden between the lines and his heart whispered. *Oh my God, she loves me.* He wanted to celebrate, to embrace her and swing her in a circle and kiss her fully, deeply and then carry her away to the…what was he thinking? Down boy, down.

"I believe in signs, Hawke. Even someone insensitive to signs should surely see through this one. While I was so preoccupied with 'just a kiss' as you so delicately put it, my daughter, my most precious Pia, disappeared. That is clearly a message. Loud and clear. That kiss was a mistake. A huge, unforgivable mistake." Her chin quivered and tears trailed down her perfect complexion. "My God! What have I done?"

He reached out to hold her but she backed away.

"I believe in signs too, Sage. Pia didn't disappear because we kissed. Sure it wouldn't have happened today, but perhaps another day. Consider this; I'm here at the Thistle Dew this weekend and you need me."

"I DON'T need you. Pia would be home if you hadn't been here this weekend."

"Are you sure? She goes to the barn alone every day doesn't she? To feed Pooh?"

Defeated, Sage sat on a stool and stared out the window. "Shouldn't you be at a meeting right now?"

Kristen stopped at the door, hesitant to interrupt but spoke when Sage paused, "Sage, Mrs. Winters is on the phone."

A look of panic zinged across her features. Hawke knew from the old reports he'd read on microfiche that this was Eric's mother.

"You want me to talk to her?" Kristen offered.

"No, thank you. I'll take this call in my room. Excuse me. It's time for me to tell the parents of my dead husband that their only grandchild is missing."

Chapter 11

Another storm was brewing outside.

Being stranded at the Thistle Dew would have been a wonderful holiday had it not been for the ominous pallor that hovered over the Inn. Children quietly played board games while adults worked in hushed voices to solve the mystery of the missing little girl.

Sage worked feverishly at meal preparation. She had to stir and mix and wipe counters to keep her trembling hands busy. Her heart pounded in the same painful throbbing beat as the headache behind her eyes. To top it off, her morning coffee threatened to come up. As it was, the half bagel Ruthie convinced her to eat settled like an anchor in the pit of her stomach.

With Kristen's help, Sage prepared a buffet dinner. A variety of vegetable dishes as well as a turkey with all the trimmings was plenty of food for everyone.

All during the preparation of the feast, Sage silently prayed for the phone to ring or for someone to come through the door with news of Pia.

Eric's parents had wanted to come instantly but the blizzard kept them as snowbound as the people at the Inn. Sage was grateful for that. She simply couldn't face their grief again. Especially when losing Pia was her fault. If only she'd not kissed Hawke.

When the last item had been placed on the buffet table and she was satisfied at the presentation, Sage retreated into the privacy of kitchen.

"Kristen," Sage spoke to her helper. "Please tell the guests and the writers in the lounge that dinner is served and they can dish up now."

Kristen trotted off to do her bidding.

Sage went into her private quarters, closed the door between it and the kitchen and knelt to pick up a pair of Pia's princess pajamas discarded near the sofa. Sage dropped onto the couch, and let her pent up fears release. The tears that had been threatening for hours surfaced, bubbling over as she sobbed uncontrollably into the clothes of the child she loved more than life itself.

She was so absolutely sure that Pia would be home by now. Eric came to her in a dream and told her so.

But maybe he was angry. Maybe he was angry at her for kissing Hawke and losing Pia. Maybe he took Pia away, maybe Pia was not kidnapped but lost outside in this horrible snowstorm, frozen. Dead.

"Please Eric, no, I'm so sorry. Please keep Pia safe and warm and... Eric, please I can't lose her too. I'm sorry I kissed Hawke. I love you Eric, only you. Forever. I won't ever let that happen again."

Hawke had quietly opened the door to be with Sage. He watched her in silence, the excruciating pain tearing her heart into shreds like a paper Valentine's Day card. He knew the pain, identified with it; although his son was not missing he had been taken away by his ex-wife and the missing was painful.

He thought of Luke now and the aching black void his son's absence created. And this was so similar, so painful. A wound that would never heal. Maybe this was worse. He knew Luke was safe and happy with his mother in France. Pia was missing. Maybe cold, maybe scared, maybe lost. Maybe dead.

"Sage." Hawke took a tentative step toward her.

"Is there news?" She looked hopefully, her eyes begging him to nod.

"Not yet."

"Then go, Please."

"I want to be here for you." He went to her side, "As a friend."

"We crossed that line at the barn." She closed her eyes to suppress a nagging headache. "That kiss was not the kiss of friends."

"I know." His mouth felt dry.

"I love Eric." She whimpered.

"I know." He sat beside her.

The escalating roar and sudden quiet outside signaled that someone had arrived on a snowmobile. Three unidentifiable snow covered creatures stepped into the kitchen through the back door shivering and stomping snow onto Sage's once clean floor.

She hurried into the kitchen. Sage recognized Peter as he unwrapped a scarf from around his face.

Simultaneously they asked, "Any word yet?"

Simultaneously they each shook their heads in disappointment, "No, nothing."

Danny and Lowell, the other two snow mobilers, removed their gloves.

"Do you know where I've been all gawdamned day?" Lowell hung his wet jacket on a coat hook above the radiator. "I've been treated like a gawdamned kidnapper that's what. Whose idea was it, Sage, to make me look like the guilty party?" Lowell accused. "I noticed the writer didn't get hauled down to the station for questioning. Seems to me anyone who'd be able to write a whole gawdamned book about a kidnapping may have perfected a plan. Has anyone thought of that, Chief?" Lowell removed his hat and shook the wet from his hair spraying the counters with disregard.

"Hawke was with Sage." Peter explained, "They were walking back from the pond and Pia ran on ahead." Peter looked at Sage for confirmation. She nodded.

"And I just happen to find Pia's mitten next to my truck in the parking area and I'm guilty."

"You found Pia's mitten?" Sage looked at Peter.

"We were keeping quiet, in case a kidnapper made contact."

Sage went to Lowell and touched his sleeve. "I knew it wasn't you, Lowell. I told them you would never do anything to hurt Pia or me." She spoke softly, soothing his wounds, "You were Eric's friend and he's trusting you to help keep us safe. Right?"

His anger frightened her. She began to have serious doubts about his innocence. She hoped by appealing to his sense of loyal friendship to Eric, he would tell her that Pia was safe. That is... if he knew.

"You think I took her?" He looked at her with venom, shook his arm free from her clasp.

Sage shook her head. "No, Lowell I don't."

"Good, because I did MY homework." He smirked at the chief of police. "Did you check out the writer, Hawke?" He scanned the room. The others waited, "Well I did! He doesn't even have his picture on any of his book jackets. Don't you find that suspicious? I kept digging until I came across an old television interview from the PBS station. It doesn't even look like the same man."

"What are you suggesting?" Sage asked confused by this new information.

"I don't think this man is the author, Hawke." Lowell nearly crowed the revelation. "He's an imposter." He whispered.

Sage almost laughed out loud. "Don't you think the other authors on the writer's board would have noticed?"

Lowell's excitement clouded his common sense, "Maybe they're all in on it." His voice lowered in a conspiring tone.

"Are you serious?" Sage shook her head in amazement.

"Lowell, I'm sorry, I just don't have the energy to listen to this."

Lowell grew angrier by the minute. "Yeah? Who searched his room? I'll bet he's not the big hero he's let you think he is." Lowell stormed out of the kitchen into the great room.

"I'll just keep an eye on him." Danny followed Lowell up the stairs.

"Peter, have you heard anything?" Sage's pleading eyes begged him to say yes.

He shook his head, "I'm sorry."

The silence that echoed in the room for nearly five minutes was broken by Lowell's loud intrusion. "See, Peter! What'd I tell you?" He held a packet of syringes in front of Peter's face.

Danny walked into the room moments later with Hawke.

Peter clearly looked amused, while Sage studied him with accusation.

"And to think I kissed you." Sage stared at Hawke, trying to see the evil in him that the syringe portrayed. "I trusted you."

"You kissed him?" Lowell shouted. "Are you serious? You don't even know this man." He stood beside Sage draping a protective arm over her shoulders.

"I'm a diabetic." Hawke explained looking at only her. He turned to Peter, "I have a vial of insulin in the film canister in the refrigerator."

Peter took the small black container from the shelf on the refrigerator door, opened it and tipped it so the vial fell into his palm. Satisfied, he returned the vial to its place.

"But the writer Hawke is a skinny geek. I saw it on TV." Lowell hated to admit defeat. "This guy doesn't even wear glasses."

"Lasik surgery."

"Buck teeth." Lowell described the old Hawke in bits and pieces. "Skinny."

"Braces. Also I worked out every day for a year in a gym with a trainer."

"Okay, I've heard enough." Peter interrupted Lowell's interrogation.

Hawke gave Sage an unfathomable look and left the room.

Once again she felt bereft. She tried not to cry. "It's just that I am so desperate to have her home. Where could she be, Lowell? Where could she be?"

Lowell opened his arms and Sage walked right into them.

Chapter 12

In the dining room the conversation was quiet yet constant. Adults still speculated on the whereabouts of little Pia while at another table, the children talked about movies, TV shows and music.

The authors sat at a table in the lounge finishing up business discussions that they worked on.

Hawke, more focused on the search for Pia than the writers' business, finally sat down with a plate full of food.

"I'm sorry to have missed some of the meeting today. This has been such a nightmare." He combed fingers through his hair, reiterating his frustration and concern.

"Have a seat, boy," Andreas pulled out a chair beside his and Hawke sat down heavily. "We've gotten most of our business attended to but we do need to know the current status of the Unseen Scene contest. How has that been going?"

"I think you'll be pleased." Hawke took a drink before continuing. "Norman has put together scoring sheets that are not only efficient for the evaluators, but I believe they will be a valuable tool for the writer. They are extremely positive and non-critical as well as offering an honest, professional critique. I have a rough hard copy for each of you to assess. We will review any suggestions and comments you have to offer and then have a final copy prepared by contest deadline." As he drank heartily from his water glass he scanned the dining room. "Where is Maribelle?"

"She is taking a light meal in her room." Andreas offered.

"She has a headache." Dakota added.

"How is Norman? He never misses a meeting. Is everything all right?" Dakota inquired as he heaped more mashed potatoes on his plate.

"He planned on being here," Hawke began, his tone reflective of his affection and respect for the old man. "But called Kristen at the last minute to say that his wife had taken a turn for the worse and he would be at the nursing home if we needed to get in touch with him."

"Poor old guy." Kristen heard the last as she came in to refill water glasses.

"Yeah." Dakota agreed, "Has she been sick for a long time?"

"About thirty—two years." Hawke answered. "Almost his whole married life."

"What happened to her?" Kristen, intrigued with this story of tragic love, sat in a vacant chair.

"A car accident wasn't it?" Andreas asked.

"Yes. She was driving. Their daughter was killed in that accident. I guess she just never came out of it. A combination of guilt and grief, Norman said."

Hawke remembered the night of a few too many whiskey sours when Norman broke down and related that terrible event, sobbing openly to his friend. "He's always claimed that Emily was his muse. She's the one he dedicates his books to."

"His wife?"

"No. Emily was his daughter."

"Are you serious? I never knew that. Poor Norman."

"We'll send him a card or something."

"He'll appreciate that." Hawke ate quickly, excused himself and returned to the kitchen to check on Sage.

He found her in Lowell's embrace, sobbing uncontrollably. Lowell cast Hawke the smug look of victory.

On the other side of the room, Peter toyed with the broken putter and spoke softly on the phone. He hung up and signaled to Danny to leave.

"I'd like to go over the lists again." Hawke spoke to Peter when the police chief replaced the phone on its holder. "I can't help but think we've missed something."

Sage stopped crying. She stepped away from Lowell. Her red-rimmed eyes glared at him with fury.

"A thousand phone calls have been made. There is an Amber Alert out and everyone in town is freezing their butts off looking for her." Her voice accelerated, quivered, and finally broke. "My God, Hawke, the police are doing everything humanly possible. Where is she? Do you think you can write a happy ending to this real life mystery? I wish you could. Can you please write me an ending that places my beautiful little girl in my arms?"

He said nothing, knowing she needed to let some of the grief and anger out.

Tears streamed down her cheeks. "You live in a fictional world where you control the endings. You can make your characters happy. You have no control over this. This is real life. This is reality. You are not the hero of this story!" Her voice reflected the strain of the past two days. "You're even a made-over version of yourself. Everything about you is fiction." She reached for more tissues. "Get out of here, please."

Her words caused him to flinch as if her palm slapped hard across his face. Hawke closed his eyes, inhaled slowly and turned to the Chief.

"Peter, I'd like to look over the lists again." Hawke insisted, appealing to the police chief.

Peter gathered the sheets of printed register and handed them to Hawke.

"We've missed something." Hawke reiterated. He studied the fragile young mother. Today she reminded him of a small glass bird his mother kept on her keepsake shelf. It was the only one of her treasures he caught and prevented from shattering when his new step—father threw him against the wall in a fit of anger.

Lowell looked ready to remove him physically if Hawke didn't comply.

Hawke took the papers and went through the door. It physically pained him to know that she held their kiss to blame. A knife pierced his heart with every inhale. Heartache. He knew nothing would take this pain away.

Her soul must hurt, too. She suffered from a heartache that could not be matched. A child lost. A mother without answers. The not knowing would be the pointed blade that repeatedly pierced her heart.

"You too, Lowell. I just want to be alone."

Hawke heard Sage's words and caught the angry look Lowell wore. He didn't like the handyman, but Sage's unconscious dismissal had to hurt. He almost felt sorry for Lowell. Almost.

Sage ran into the bathroom and as he passed by he heard her being sick. It took every ounce of self-control to not burst through the door and hold her until her grief and terror was assuaged. But he walked away with the papers, knowing he needed to find Pia rather than comfort Sage. That would bring more happiness than any other thing he could do.

In his room, Hawke read and reread each entry. Many of the guests visited frequently and since they had all been contacted and accounted for he reviewed one-timers.

Peter's small police force and a number of volunteers had jotted notes as they solicited responses. Although most of the people were sincerely concerned for Pia's welfare, no one could provide any valuable information or clues to finding her.

Tormented by this apparent failure, Hawke became plagued by haunting memories of his youth. A dismal failure in the eyes of his step-father when he proved to be too gangly and uncoordinated to be an athlete and too fanciful to be a scholar. The daily chorus of 'loser' rang in Hawke's ears. Tears formed in his eyes and the determination spawned of fear and hatred motivated him to go over the lists again. He categorized and classified, eliminated and highlighted searching for the elusive clue.

Nothing, nothing.

"What did you think? It would flash in neon lights?" He reprimanded himself for his impatience.

He carried the colorful papers down to the office area behind the large oak reception desk, where he found Kristen talking on the phone.

"Oh, um, Robbie, I have to go. I'll talk to you later." She put the receiver back in its holder and turned to Hawke. "Is there news?"

"No, not yet. I want to ask you a few questions."

"Sure." She motioned him to sit in the other desk chair.

"I've listed a few people I need to know more about. Will you help me?"

Kristen studied the list. They were all recurring visitors and she knew a little about each of them. "These people. These are all kind people. What exactly are you looking for?"

"Motive." He shifted in his seat to look at the abbreviated list with her. "Is there anyone here who is needy? Lonely? Mourning the death of a loved one?" Is here anyone here that you could imagine in a wild moment might kidnap a child?"

She began to read the names, making personal

comments for each person, each couple.

"They're all good people, Hawke!" Kristin rubbed her brow in frustration. "I'd trust my child with any of them, if I had a baby."

"And Norman? He never mention to me that he came back here after the writers weekend last fall." Hawke talked with the elderly man weekly. "I see he was here three times in November."

"He called it respite," Kristen said. "He came on Saturdays. He just kept to his room, resting and I assume writing. He likes to read stories to Pia. She calls him Papa Norman."

"He's a harmless enough old goat."

Danny knocked lightly then entered the small space. "Hawke, Peter wants to see you."

Hawke followed Danny into the kitchen. The men were covered with snow and had apparently just come in.

"Where's Sage?" Hawke wondered if she needed him. But then he remembered her icy cold dismissal and knew she would always blame their kiss on Pia's disappearance.

"The doctor gave her a sedative. She's sleeping." Peter spoke quietly. "Listen we just had a call that scared the hell out of me. A 911 call reported a garbage bag tossed into the ditch at the end of Rabbit Road."

Hawke felt his pulse accelerate, his stomach clench like a fist.

"Thank God, it was nothing. Just a bag of trash." Peter looked as if that call and its resulting investigation had completely unnerved him. His hand trembled as he took a glass of water Danny handed to him. "Danny and I are going back to the station. Let us know if you hear anything."

"I will."

Peter hesitated a moment and then seemed to come to a decision. "Could you just look in on her once in a while?"

Hawke nodded. He understood how much it cost Peter to make the request of a possible suspect. The question gave Hawke mental permission to do exactly what he intended to do anyway.

Hawke turned towards her rooms when they left.

The room was dark, save for a small glow from a nightlight by her dresser. She lay on her side, arms wrapped around a pillow. He reached down and brushed away a wisp of hair that teased her cheek with each puff of her breath. He longed to lie down beside her, hold her and promise her that everything would be all right.

Convinced that Sage slept soundly, he walked quietly to leave the room. She mumbled, whimpered, cried out as if she were in physical pain. Hawke hurried to her side, sat beside her and stroked her hair to calm her. Lost in her nightmares, Sage reached out and pulled him closer. He adjusted his position to accommodate her need. He held her closely, breathing in the fragrance of her shampoo, savoring the softness of her sleeping form, trying to send her comfort, strength and courage through his embrace. His heart beat rhythmically, steadily, aching in empathy as he rocked her gently murmuring prayers of promise. As her restlessness quieted, Hawke closed his eyes to savor the feelings emanating from her fathomable faith.

He nodded off momentarily and only noticed his uncomfortable posture when a chill woke him with a shiver. He carefully laid Sage back onto her bed, brought the quilt to her chin, touched his lips to her hair and slipped out of the room.

Once upstairs, Hawke couldn't sleep, but his body demanded that he lie horizontal for a few hours. He closed his eyes. His brain raced, swirling like brown leaves in a backyard whirlwind. The dizziness calmed itself until he sat up to drink a glass of water.

He closed his eyes for a second and saw her in his dreams giggling as she read a story, her eyes twinkling with mischief.

"Pia?" he called softly. "Where are you, honey?" He scootched back down to let his head rest on the pillow. "Your Mommy's sick with worry, little one. Can't you help us bring you home?"

SLAP!! Hawke snapped awake. Had he dozed off? What woke him? A POP! Not like a cap gun or champagne cork. He rolled to his side to scan the room. A hardcover book rested innocently on the hardwood floor about a foot from the dresser. Hawke glanced at the door. He hadn't heard anyone enter. A shiver traveled up his spine as he noticed the cover. A Ghost of a Chance by Norman Stevens. Norman's latest book.

"Norman?" Hawke hurried to the door and checked the hallway expecting to see the old man doubled over in a fit of laughter. It would be just like him to try to bring out the timid, frightened man that Hawke had cast away months ago with his coke bottle glasses, blue plastic pocket protector and Velcro sneakers. But there was no one in the hallway except a cold breath of air.

Sleep was impossible. His head throbbed as it someone were pounding on the door to his mind. Thirst. He needed to give himself an injection. How many hours had it been? Maybe he had hallucinated because his blood sugar was off kilter. The book was not a hallucination. He carried it down stairs to the kitchen where he promptly took care of his medical needs, drank two tall glasses of water, then reread the book jacket while he placed a mug of water in the microwave. No more coffee, he admonished himself. *That might be why I am so wired.*

Hawke had read the book, proofed it and even

worked with Norman on the query which was basically used as the blurb on the back cover. He flipped it open, studied the old man's photo and skimmed through his accolades. He flipped through the first few pages and stopped to read the nearly indecipherable chicken scratch. To Sage with warmest affection.

How sweet. But how did this book end up in my room? On my floor? He played with the tea bag, dipping it while this mind wandered through all possibilities.

"Okay", he spoke aloud to the empty room, "Kristen was reading this book while working upstairs this morning, set the book down on the foot of my bed. I didn't notice it when I went to bed and kicked it to the floor in my sleep." Yes, that made complete sense. Whew! For a minute there he thought he was losing it.

Then at the precise moment when he felt relief, assured that he was not crazy, the blue flowered golf ball fell from its perch on the display shelf and hit the floor with a solid ping, followed by tiny echoing bumps. Then it rolled across the floor and beneath the door of the pantry.

Too stunned to move, Hawke stared for a second at the place the golf ball disappeared, then let his eyes retrace its fall and travel line. He waited for someone to jump out from the refrigerator and yell "BOO!" But the room remained exceedingly quiet. He suddenly noticed the wind died down, had stopped its incessant howling and rattling of shutters. The blizzard was over.

Chapter 13

Somewhat unnerved, Hawke took a sip of his tea, then strode over to the pantry. He had never been brave, although his mother told him he was because he gave his own insulin shots without complaint. Bravery didn't come with his new image. Not like he wore tights and a cape. Bravery had not been counseled into him, although his shrink helped fight the demons.

He put his hand on the doorknob, which felt unearthly cold, pausing to summon up courage. If someone was hiding in the pantry, it had better be in jest. Because if anyone was out to hurt Sage any more than she already was he'd, well, he didn't know what he would do but it wouldn't be pretty.

*One, two, three! H*e yanked the door open and scanned the food closet quickly. It was empty. A movement caught his eye. Down by his foot, the blue flowered golf ball rolled ever so slightly. He must have kicked it. Nothing else seemed to be out of place. Dishes, glasses, a blender; all in their labeled places.

As he turned to leave, a glimpse of colors on the bottom shelf, not in harmony with the kitchen utensils, canned goods and paper supplies, stopped him. He bent down to retrieve the misplaced object.

It was a book. One of Pia's books. He studied the cover. A pig, a little girl and a spider.

Charlotte's Web.

He left the pantry with his treasures. A child's book and a blue flowered golf ball. Confusion clouded his consciousness for a second as he set the ball gingerly back in its place on the carefully constructed display shelf. How had the ball jumped out of the hole that kept it from rolling off the shelf? Hawke could not find a feasible explanation.

A half hour later he still sat at the counter, drinking cold tea, searching the pages of the two books alternately. There was a message here.

Somewhere.

****

Yes yes yes!!!!!! Eric shouted to Hawke. I've done all I can except draw you a map.

Think.

Yes, sleep on it. You'll see the connections in your dreams. Pia's fine. She's safe and warm, although she IS ready to come home.

****

He was running on a treadmill chasing after Pia whose gray chair zoomed like a hovercraft just out of his reach. "Pia," he tried to call to her but no sound came as he chased her down.

He studied the vision in his mind, down a long, clean, white corridor. A hospital? He followed a large brown spider into a dimly lit room. He read Pia's name in it's web. Suddenly a bright overhead light went on. He was forced to squint until his eyes adjusted. Then he saw her.

Hawke awoke in a sweat.

He went downstairs and into Sage's private quarters and to her bedroom. His large hand gently smoothed her hair from her forehead.

"Sage." He whispered in a half hearted attempt to wake her up. "Sage, honey. Can you wake up?"

The sedative the doctor had given her last night was still at work. She didn't even stir. He tucked Pia's book beneath her pillow, touched his lips to a delightful little dimple by the corner of her mouth and decided to follow his instincts.

Although it was only four o'clock in the morning,

Hawke needed to get Pia. He returned to the kitchen and called Peter who arrived in the patrol car fifteen minutes later. The car was already warm and they left in the quiet dark of very early morning.

Here we come, little Pia. Here we come. Hawke whispered to the little girl in a prayer.

The roads were clear of both traffic and weather. Plows had cleaned up efficiently after the blizzard, leaving behind snow banks taller than most men.

Hawke and Peter were quiet, each lost in his own thoughts, each anticipating the outcome of this journey.

Peter turned the radio on to an all night country western station. The music filled the car with hope, patriotism, love and humor. It seemed to take the edge off of the anxiety seated inconspicuously between the men. They stopped once for coffee.

A normally two hour trip took less and sometime later in a very small, secluded town they found an all night gas station and asked directions to the Winter Garden Nursing Home.

There were few lights on inside the nursing home, the door was locked and the nurse on duty was clearly unnerved by their arrival.

"We're looking for Norman Stevens. Is he here?"

She hesitated, worry crossing her otherwise stoic features. "Yes. God bless him." she led them down a gray and antiseptic hall. "He hasn't left her side. Especially after the miracle this weekend."

Hawke glanced at Peter, knowing a revelation was coming, feeling the instinctual call of the mystery about to be solved. Warmth radiated in his soul.

"Mrs. Stevens spoke for the first time in more than thirty years." She stood outside the door to a patient's room. "She smiled too. I'm sure it was because Emily, their grand daughter, is visiting."

Hawke's heart suffused with love, and sheer

blessed relief. Followed by concern for his friend, Norman. He'd noticed that Norman was getting more forgetful lately, but he still wrote well. Then again, he'd read studies that suggested people lost different functions when dementia set in. Or perhaps Norman simply had a small stroke that heralded memory loss and he simply forgot to tell Sage he'd taken Pia for a visit.

As they entered the room Hawke noticed first the little girl curled up at the foot of the bed, carefully covered and comfortable.

His whole body relaxed and he had to grab the foot of the hospital bed. Pia's blonde head was only inches from his hand. He reached out and touched her, need filling his heart as his fingers made sure she was real. Wisps of hair feathered across his hand, much like her mother's. His soul floated, and then settled as he cupped her little cheek and bent to kiss her forehead.

Norman slept in a chair pulled close to the bed. His head rested on the blanket by his wife's hip. With a gentle grasp he held his wife's fragile hand near his lips. His left arm stretched across the mattress, his hand buried beneath the bottom of the blanket that covered Pia. The nurse lifted the corner of the blanket for the men to see that Norman lovingly held Pia's bare foot. His thumb moved rhythmically back and forth on her soft instep.

Have they been here the entire weekend?" Peter whispered, outwardly affected by the scene. "When did they get here?"

"They arrived Saturday night with hamburgers and French fries and had a picnic on her bed." The nurse smiled affectionately at the slumbering trio. "Emily is such a sweet little girl."

"Can I talk to you for a minute out in the hall?" Peter nodded toward the door and the clearly confused nurse acquiesced.

Norman stirred, snored loudly, kissed his wife's hand and with a satisfied sigh drifted off back to sleep.

Hawke hated to wake them. Hated to disrupt this moment for Norman. His old friend and respected colleague slipped into unreality. What would this mean for the old codger? Jail? Hawke hoped that could be avoided. This weekend had been pure hell for so many people, especially Sage. He thought of Sage now.

"Norman." Hawke spoke softly trying not to startle him. He touched the old guy's shoulder. "Norman, wake up."

Norman awoke slowly. He checked his wife, kissed her fingers, then looked over at Pia. He turned and noticed Hawke.

"Hello, Hawke."

He rose with difficulty, steadying himself on the arm of the chair. "Mattie spoke to me." His voice was rough from sleep. "She smiled and said that she loved me." Tears clouded his vision. "I've waited more than thirty years for her to speak to me." He looked affectionately at her. Then he looked at Pia. "It was Emily. She worked a miracle."

"Norman," Hawke worried about Norman's delusions. "Emily is..."

"Shhhh." Norman pressed a wrinkled index finger to his lips. "Please don't let Mattie hear you." His rheumy eyes filled with tears. "I've waited all these years to hear her sweet voice. I come here every day. I sing to her, read her my manuscripts, the newspaper, articles about people she knew. I've played her records. We used to dance you know. Won a contest doing the Charleston. Did you know that?"

Hawke shook his head. No he hadn't heard that one. He heard so many memories during their professional friendship. He had always felt so sad for the brilliant man who lived as if his wife would wake up from a nap any minute and his little daughter was only playing in the next room.

Hawke watched his friend, studying him, assessing his current demeanor. Norman's hand had a slight tremor, his cheeks looked unusually ruddy and his voice was raspy when he spoke.

When had Norman become such a frail, old man?

On the bed Pia whimpered and changed position, stretching one leg so that her little foot poked out from beneath the blanket. Norman moved quickly, tenderly tucking the blanket beneath the cherished child.

"We need to take Pia home to her mother." Hawke watched Norman's brows knit together, the old man's eyes flitting from his wife's gentle, sleeping form to the little girl curled up at the foot of the bed.

Hawke could see when reality suddenly crawled into Norman's mind, his body trembled and he crumbled into the plastic chair.

"Oh, my God." Norman voice quivered, "What have I done?" He shook his head as if the motion would stir his mixed-up brain cells. "I pulled into the parking area at Thistle Dew. We had an authors meeting. And I saw her, Emily, in her pretty snowsuit, cheeks all rosy from the cold."

Peter and the nurse entered the room quietly, but Norman didn't notice, as he related his story.

"She was excited to see me and gave me a hug and I asked her if she wanted to go for a ride and she nodded and climbed in the car." He took a wrinkled linen handkerchief from his pocket and wiped tears from his eyes. "Poor Sage. I should call her and explain." He tried to rise but his knees resisted and he sat again.

"Sage has been worried, Norman." Hawke's compassion for the old man reflected in his voice.

"She doesn't know where Pia is."

Norman nodded. "I never would hurt Pia or Sage." He shook his head in disbelief. "I'm so sorry. She'll never forgive me."

A tiny gravely voice piped up from the bed, "Mr. Hawke? Uncle Pete? I knew you'd come. Is Mommy here?" Her eyes darted around the room.

"Are you ready to go home?" Hawke lifted her into his arms. "She's waiting there."

Pia nodded enthusiastically then looked down at Norman who sat quietly studying his own clasped hands. She wriggled until Hawke let her down. Pia took two barefoot steps and climbed onto the old man's lap. "We made her happy with our surprise didn't we, Papa Norman?" She wrapped her little arms around his neck and squeezed. "I'll ask Mommy if we can come back to visit real soon. Okay?"

Tearfully ashamed, Norman silently nodded.

Chapter 14

Pia talked incessantly for the first half hour. "Did Papa Norman call you? Papa Norman bought me an ice cream cone. A chocolate one. In the winter!" She looked out the car window at the town just waking. "How'd you know where I was, Mr. Hawke?"

Hawke handed her a crumpled piece of paper from his pocket and held it out.

She unfolded it slowly and screeched with delight when she saw the little white feather. "My Daddy told you that I went with Papa Norman."

Hawke nodded, still unsure of the justification of the sequence of events early that morning.

Fifteen minutes later she finally slept contentedly for the rest of the trip home.

Peter pulled the cruiser up the long driveway to Thistle Dew. A voice came over his police radio requesting his immediate attention back in town. He pulled in to a space beside the freshly shoveled, banked path to the front door. "I wish I could go in to see her expression, but duty calls."

Hawke lifted the groggy child from the back seat.

Pia whimpered then snuggled deep into his shoulder as they headed toward the house.

By the kitchen window, several little birds flittered around a nearly empty bird feeder as the sun chased the dismal gray pallor from the sky.

His footfalls on the wooded porch sounded thunderous in the early morning quiet. Hawke opened the door and entered the empty hall.

"You're home, little Pia." he whispered into her disheveled curls. "Wake up, Sweetheart."

The little girl stirred, groaned her reluctance and stretched, then settled once again into the comfort of the big man's shoulder.

"Your Mom will be so happy to see you." He carried her to the kitchen and paused at the doorway leading to the private area. Pia straightened, rubbed the sleep from her eyes with chubby fists and smiled at Hawke.

"Will Mommy be surprised?" She whispered with a gleam in her eye.

Hawke nodded and touched his lips to her forehead.

"Yes, she will. She really missed you a lot." He hefted Pia to his other hip, entered Sage's living room and stopped at the master bedroom door. He was not prepared for the scene that greeted him.

Lowell sat in an armchair positioned close to Sage's side, holding tight to her limp hand.

Hawke felt rage gnaw on his insides. Hawke should have suspected Lowell was here since the path from parking area to porch had been shoveled. The scene unnerved him.

At the sight of her mother, Pia wiggled, a signal for Hawke to let her down.

"Mommy?" As Pia scampered over to the big bed, Lowell stood and scooped her up. Pia, clearly focused on her mother's sleeping form, wiggled desperately to be released. "Mommy!" Her demand to be let go in the single cry.

****

Sometime during the night the storm had quieted, but the last traces of a north wind rattled a loose shutter on her bedroom window. She'd have to ask Lowell to fix it when things calmed down. When Pia came home. She looked at the blackness outside her window. Still dark. Still night. Still a nightmare.

A place on her cheek felt hot as if she had been burned. She gently touched the spot near her mouth. It felt like a tiny glimmer of sunshine. It was definitely a comforting warmth. She laid back and smiled. It was a good sign.

"Today Pia." she whispered. "Please come home today."

Sage closed her eyes as tears once again threatened. She rolled to her side and tucked her hands under her pillow. That was strange. She felt the cool smoothness of a book. She didn't remember putting a book under her pillow when she made the bed in the morning. She glanced at her night stand to see if the book she had been reading was still there. It was just as she had left it before Pia disappeared. How many days ago?

Perplexed, she pulled the book out from its hiding place and gasped. Her immediate response was to drop it like a match whose flame had reached her fingers. But instead she clutched it to her chest. Her mind raced with possible explanations. None seemed plausible. It seemed as if the book were trying to tell her something.

Charlotte's Web was Pia's favorite story. She studied the cover. A smiling spider, a smiling pig and a smiling little girl.

"What are you trying to tell me?" She spoke to the book then quickly scanned the room to reassure herself that she was alone. Sleep had been a welcomed companion during the night, but now she was awake for the day. Today would be the day. She felt sure of it.

Tonight Pia would sleep in her own bed.

It was sometime later, when the howling outside ceased and the sky only hinted at morning, she dreamt. She and Eric were playing hide and seek with Pia. She'd see Pia peek out from behind a tree but when she ran to the tree, Pia wouldn't be there.

Sage mewled with frustration, called out to Pia but the giggling imp was ever elusive. At one point in her dream, she and Eric were chasing Pia, who like a little purple butterfly, skittered across a field of daisies.

Eric reached out and took Sage's hand, but he felt cold and although she tried to pull away he held her firmly in his grasp.

Too weak to resist, she wondered why she did not feel the comfort typical in Eric's hand.

"Mommy."

Sage heard Pia calling, her voice distant and tiny.

A movement of purple caught her eye. There, in the corner of the doorframe of the alpaca barn, a purple butterfly struggled to escape from the sticky silk of a spider's web.

"Mommy!" It's little voice called again. But this time louder, clearer.

"I'm coming." Her mind called out as it plodded through a dense fog in her brain. She opened her heavy lidded eyes and saw a blur of colors, a wiggling blur of purple and gold, blinked again and the fog cleared.

Pia struggled to be released from Lowell's firm hold.

"Pia?" she cried out to her daughter.

Was this still a dream? Was she only being teased by the nightmare?

Sage reached and Pia nearly jumped from Lowell's grasp, onto the bed and into her mother's waiting hug.

"Here she is." Lowell proudly released his prize on the bed beside her mother and nearly glowed as Sage cast him a grateful glance.

"Mommy, don't cry." Pia wiped tears from her mother's face, "I'm home now."

"These are happy tears." Sage nuzzled her

daughter, reveling in her still baby smells and her soft skin. "Are you hurt?" Sage began a quick visual check-up looking for tell-tale signs of abuse. She shuddered to think her daughter had been mistreated.

Pia only squiggled and giggled at her mother's ministrations, "You're silly, Mommy. Papa Norman wouldn't hurt me."

She looked past Pia and saw Lowell.

"You were with Norman?" Sage asked, puzzled.

Lowell closed his eyes with an affirmative nod. He offered Sage a thin smile as he backed quietly into the kitchen and exhaled a sigh of relief.

With a confidence borne of dumb luck, Lowell reached into the cupboard for a mug. He needed a cup of coffee.

He set the mug on the counter and just happened to glance into the cup before pouring. A feather. A downy white feather rested on the bottom of the mug. "Damn pigeons!" He carried it to the trash to drop it in. It stuck to his finger and when he shook his fingers the feather detached. Lowell tried to grab it but instead made a current of air that lifted the feather causing it to float up, zig zagging just above Lowell's reach.

Lowell stood watching the feather with both fascination and fear. The feather caught in a draft by the back door, danced and floated and finally fluttered to rest on Eric's blue flowered golf ball on its plaque by the door.

"Damn." Lowell grabbed his jacket and darted outside.

****

Lowell you snake-in-the-grass. I can't believe you're actually taking the credit for finding Pia. All those years of lying and cheating your way through school, all those years of getting caught eventually...have you learned nothing?

Don't you remember your money making scheme, when you wanted to go to baseball camp? You stole Miss Vera's cat and didn't return it until you knew she was offering a reward. Don't you remember the trouble you got in when the truth got out?

I'm watching you Lowell. I'm watching you with Sage and Pia and I'm sorry to say, I don't like what I see.

I'll have to help Sage see the truth here. Hawke is a really great guy. He's the guy I would like to see as a permanent fixture in Sage and Pia's life.

Now, if only I can convince Sage of that.

Chapter 15

It didn't take long for word of Pia's safe return home to spread through the small community and before the first pot of coffee had brewed, friends and family gathered in the great room.

Pia enjoyed the special attention, hugs, stuffed animals, dolls and books brought by friends in celebration of her safe return.

Dr. Douglas arrived in a flurry of importance, took Pia and Sage into their private quarters and gently examined Pia as he asked questions about her purple bunny and Pooh. Sprinkled in between were questions about Norman and Mattie.

Sage caught his slight nod that all was well with her child and sagged inwardly with relief.

They returned to the party in the great room, with friends, neighbors and guests passing Pia around for hugs and kisses.

Lowell swallowed up praise and slaps on the back greedily. With each retelling of the rescue, Lowell portrayed Norman as a little more belligerent and himself more heroic.

"Lowell, could you please add a couple of logs to the fire? Some of the guests have commented on being chilly." Sage touched his shoulder before interrupting his account of Pia's rescue.

"I'm busy here, Sage." Lowell said. He dismissed her and continued. "Now where was I?"

"I'll take care of the fire, Sage." Danny moved towards the stack of dry wood, hefted two split logs and watched the shower of sparks fly as he laid the logs on the hot coals.

"Thank you." Sage searched Lowell's face for another glimpse of the hero she had seen a few hours ago.

All traces were gone. The same old self-centered, rude Lowell continued his conversation without a second glance at Sage.

After a few hours, Lowell's storytelling became a bit more animated, he made Norman out to be a bit more senile and poor little Pia wavering on the brink of danger.

Lowell sat in Eric's recliner, like a king on his throne, glowing in the attention as the peasants gathered round. "I knew the old coot was dangerous first time I met him."

Kristen rolled her eyes.

"Peter will do the world a favor to have that old man locked up for good." He paused to take a swig of beer. As he raised the bottle to his mouth, it tipped ever so slightly, until the amber liquid poured onto his lap, wetting his khaki pants in a very discomfiting area.

Lowell jumped up, his face white. Beating a hasty retreat and murmuring something about being late for work, he almost ran from the room.

A few people laughed at his mishap, then drifted to where Pia held court in the bay window, surrounded by her purple bunny and other stuffed toys.

Outside an ominous roll of thunder echoed from the mountain and rattled the windows. Most of the well-wishers in the great room were so absorbed in conversation that it went unnoticed.

Ruthie placed another tray of cookies on the sideboard in the great room, just as Sage finished setting up the urn for more coffee.

"Kristin had fun baking in your kitchen today." Ruthie noted.

"I've let her help out before, but I never realized

how good she is in a crisis. I might promote her off the desk job and into helping me. We're getting booked more and more for cozy conferences and even weekend parties from the townsfolk."

"Oh, that is so wonderful, Sage." Ruthie gave a soft smile. "Eric would be so proud of you. He always said you were stronger than you ever imagined."

"Thank you." Sage felt the well of tears sparkle on her lashes, but she swallowed them down. This was a day of rejoicing. Somehow, she knew Eric kept Pia safe.

"Peter should be here soon." Ruthie told Sage.

"Thank you for helping me, Ruthie."

"It was no problem at all." Ruthie gave her a winsome smile and moved towards the foyer as Peter came in, brushing a hand through already disheveled hair.

The locals were already calling it a day and everyone was putting on jackets and mittens to brave the winter weather.

Pia yawned widely and waved to the children going out with their parents.

As the door closed on the last guest, Sage went back into the great room and dropped into a chair.

Pia was curled in her mother's lap.

Peter came from the kitchen with a mug of coffee. He sat down with a relieved sigh in the peaceful quiet.

Ruthie sat next to him and kicked off her shoes.

"Had a busy day?" Peter reached over and smoothed the curls of the sleeping child.

"A wonderful day." Sage tried to hide a yawn. Her cheeks nearly ached from smiling. "Everyone in town was here, I think." She smiled still, enveloped by the love from her caring friends.

"Ruthie and Kristen prepared nibbles and we all just milled around thankful for the miracle of Pia's safe return. So many people admitted they really feared she had wandered off in the storm. Mr. Adams said he always kept his eye out for her while he walked his dog. People have been so kind." She took a tissue from her sleeve as tears welled.

"And what about Hawke?" Peter asked.

"Hawke?" Sage stared at Peter totally perplexed. "He hasn't been here. I'd assumed he'd checked out." Her eyes swept the room. "No, I haven't seen him since yesterday, I think. My days have all blended into one long, very long nightmare."

She closed her eyes and shook her head in a feeble attempt to erase the weekend. When had she seen him last? She couldn't recall. She touched her fingertip to a sensitive spot at the corner of her lips. She no longer felt the heat, but there was a lingering tingling sensation there. Strange.

"He didn't bring Pia to you?" Peter asked, perplexed.

"I heard Pia call me, opened my eyes and Lowell was holding her. When she squirmed and called out to me he put her down beside me on the bed." She smiled as she relived that glorious moment. Sage gently kissed the crown of her sleeping child. "I didn't see Hawke at all."

"What?" Peter stared at her. "Hawke didn't bring Pia to you?"

"Lowell brought her to me." Sage nearly bubbled. "I didn't know he had it in him. Actually I didn't even know Lowell was looking for her. I had just assumed he kept to the barns." She shook her head in disbelief. "Apparently Norman had Pia all along." She changed position a little to keep her arm from falling asleep. Pia didn't stir.

"Lowell told you this?" Peter reached for a chocolate chip cookie and dunked it in his coffee. He stole a glance at Ruthie who offered him silent permission to have a sweet.

Peter's look of consternation made Sage vaguely

wondered if he'd been listening to her recount Lowell's tale. It was as if he was thinking of something else.

She brushed the thought away, thinking if Peter had something to tell her, he'd do it in his own good time.

"Pia told me she had been with Papa Norman, as she calls him. They've gotten very close over the past few months." Sage's eyes filled with tears. "Lowell says you have to arrest him. That he's dangerous. But he didn't hurt her."

"It's up to you, Sage. He did take her and he did cause you and numerous others profound worry, as well as exhaustive searching." Sage contemplated Peter's comments.

"I need to see him, speak to him. I'm sure he was just lonely." Sage's affection for the old man all but obliterated the three days of intense anxiety he had put her through.

She had Pia, safe and sound, snuggled in her arms and for Sage little else mattered. "Pia said we need to visit him. She said he was crying when she left him."

Peter nodded, "That might be a good idea." He set the empty mug on the table. "I can take you to see him if you'd like."

"Would tomorrow be all right? I don't want this weekend to scar Pia emotionally. I'd like to see if we can settle this with as little turmoil as possible, as soon as possible." She tried to stand but the added weight of her sleeping child made her efforts ineffectual.

Peter reached down and carefully lifted Pia to cradle in his arms. "Lead the way." He followed Sage to Pia's bedroom and laid her on the crisp sheet as Sage pulled down the comforter.

"Thank you, Peter, for all that you and your men have done." She gave the big man a hug. "I still can't believe that Lowell found her."

Lowell the goof, the obnoxious, pesky, rude barely tolerable friend. Now her hero. She'd have to rethink their relationship. Surely this was a sign. Maybe she should try to focus on some of Lowell's redeeming qualities. Yes, she would work on that tomorrow. Right now, she needed a long hot soak in a bubble bath, and a night of peaceful sleep.

****

The cold soaking on his lap was nothing compared to the icy grip that took hold of his wrist forcing him to spill beer onto his pants. Unnerved, unbalanced and uncertain, Lowell called in sick.

****

Thrilled that Pia was safely back home in her mother's arms, Eric hovered over the guests in the great room. All of their friends had gathered to reassure themselves of his little girl's safe return.

Where had Hawke gone? Why wasn't he here amidst the celebration? He was the one who had solved the mystery. He was the one whom people should be congratulating.

Lowell. Lowell was telling tales again. Gaining momentum with each version of his imaginary heroic rescue.

Somehow Eric needed to cool down Lowell's 'braveheart' or parts of his lap would explode like two little balloons being filled excessively with hot air.

Eric couldn't decide which was funnier, Lowell's dumbfounded expression when his own hand tipped the beer into his lap or the shocked expression when the cold beer deflated his ego, so to speak.

Eric's haunting laughter rumbled through the evening sky.

Chapter 16

"Hurry, Mommy. Hurry." Pia pulled her mother down the long sterile hall. "This way. This number." Her finger touched each brass numeral. "Two. Two. Seven. This is her number." She gently pushed the door open.

Whereas Sage stepped back, overwhelmed at seeing the fragile woman hooked up to tubes and monitors, Pia rushed right in and proceeded to climb up on the white hospital bed.

"Pia. No." Sage cautioned in a whispered reprimand. "She's sleeping." Sage took a tentative step into the room. The beeping of one monitor increased its rhythmic pattern.

"She's always sleeping, Mommy. But she knows I'm here. That's her happy beep." She cautiously maneuvered around tubes and wires, careful not to climb on the sleeping woman and leaned down to give a gentle hug. "Good Morning, Mama Mattie. I've come back."

Sage watched with fascination as her child kissed the gnarled hand that rested lifelessly on the pink and yellow patchwork comforter. "She likes kisses, Mommy, and she likes me to tell her stories." Pia giggled, "She smiled when I told her that Pooh peed on Uncle Lowell's foot."

"What!? I don't remember that." Sage felt a chuckle climb into her throat. Slightly unsettled at seeing the ministrations her four year old gave to this woman, she sat in a comfortable overstuffed chair beside the bed.

It wasn't difficult for Sage to imagine the pain

and guilt that brought Norman's wife to this place. If anything had happened to Pia, Sage knew she would have probably retreated the same way. When Eric died she spent many days in bed, too empty to think, much less maneuver through a day.

If it weren't for Pia, she might be there still, in that constant state of wishing. Wishing that the accident were only a nightmare. Wishing that she could turn back the clock and beg Eric just a little harder not to play golf. Wishing that they had made love that morning. Wishing she had not turned her head when he leaned over to kiss her goodbye. Wishing she were dead, too.

And she thought of Norman, losing not only his daughter in a car accident but his wife, too.

Such a tragedy.

Sage turned as she watched Pia's face light up. Norman, dressed as a dapper gentleman caller, entered the room.

"Emily," he nearly shouted with delight. He hurried to the bed to receive the hug Pia's outstretched arms invited. "You came back to visit us." He kissed her forehead.

"Yep" She pointed to the collection of photographs displayed on the dresser. "Who's those guys?" Pia kneeled at the foot of the bed studying the old black and white photos.

"They're pictures of Mattie and Emily and me." He went to the dresser and picked up one of the framed photos to bring it closer to Pia. "This one is us at home, and here's one from Easter Sunday. My girls sure looked pretty, didn't they?"

Pia nodded. "Where's the colors?"

"This is from a long time ago." He set the frame down. "We didn't have a camera that made color pictures." He stood quietly staring at the photographs.

"Why are they here?" Pia took her pink socks off

and threw them on the floor.

"I live here now. I have a room down the hall because there's not enough room for another bed in this room." He paused, watched the birds outside the window, "but now I get to be with Mattie all day."

"I'm glad, Papa Norman." Pia tickled Mattie's toe through the blanket. "I know Mattie is happy about THAT."

"I'm really happy that you came to visit. I thought your Mom would be too angry to ever let you visit me again." Norman shuddered with the realization of his crime and its repercussions. "Who brought you?"

His gaze swept the small room.

Hidden by the high back of the recliner, Sage slowly turned the chair so that he could see her.

When he noticed Sage his expression immediately altered and he nearly crumbled, steadying himself on the edge of the bed.

Sage rose to catch him and sensing his withdrawal, simply reached out and held him.

"I am so sorry." The old man nearly wept. He moved to sit in the chair Sage had just vacated and covered his face with his palms, fingertips pressing his eyes. "I don't know what happened." His eyes pleaded with Sage to understand. "One minute I was pulling into the parking lot at Thistle Dew to attend the writers meeting and the next thing I new my little Emily, all bundled up in her snowsuit, came running over to me. The nurse said my mind must have slipped back into the past for a moment. We came here to visit her mother." He reached over to clasp his wife's hand.

Sage couldn't speak.

"And she talked to us." Pia reported excitedly. "Didn't she, Papa Norman?" Pia climbed down from the high bed and up onto Norman's lap.

He winced as Pia bumped his arthritic knees.

She placed her little hands on each side of his face. "We made her happy, didn't we, Papa Norman?"

"Yes," he nodded, tears clouding his red rimmed eyes.

"But," Pia continued matter-of-factly, "Mommy says next time I hafta ask her permission first. Right Mommy?"

Sage nodded, not quite sure what to say. Clearly Pia had not been traumatized by the events of the weekend. Clearly, Norman was not a dangerous kidnapper. What would happen to him?

"Hawke came back later that same evening." Norman's voice quivered. "He stayed with Mattie and me until quite late." Norman looked up at Sage. "He told me how sick you were with worry," he shook his head, "and how ecstatic you were when he brought her home."

Pia scrambled off of Norman's lap and back onto the bed. "Mr. Hawke told me that he looks up to you. He's silly. He can't look up to you 'cause he's bigger than you."

"Pardon me?" Sage tried to control the dizzy whirlwind in her brain. "I don't understand. Are you sure Hawke..."

She looked up at just as Peter came into the room. He confirmed Norman's story with a satisfied smile.

"Well then, where was Lowell?" Totally confused, she turned back to Norman.

"Lowell?" Norman's face contorted with a puzzled expression. "Your handyman? Was he here?"

"No." Peter smiled at the kindly old man, then at Sage, whose face finally registered her understanding.

She nodded silently, searching her memory for any hint of Hawke's presence that morning Pia returned to her. She remembered that she awoke around six to use the bathroom, stumbled groggily to and from her bed, and Lowell sat there in the white chair as if he belonged.

He covered her and she mumbled a thank you and he said something and she fell blissfully back to sleep. The next thing she remembered was Lowell was handing Pia to her. But as the moment replayed in her mind, she watched as Pia pushed rather adamantly against his chest ordering him to put her down. What had she missed?

Then as she thought back, a wave of warmth washed over her. She reached up and tentatively touched the corner of her mouth. There was something. Something soft and lingering like the flavors of dark chocolate candy melting in her mouth. There were words spoken in his chocolate voice, a promise that allowed her to drift off into a deep, peaceful slumber.

And she had been so rude to him.

"Emm." a raspy whisper interrupted.

Norman rose to his feet with the spring of an adolescent.

"Emmie." The whisper nearly echoed in the stillness of the room.

Pia, clearly comfortable with her pretend role as Emily Stevens, positioned herself so that her face was inches from the old woman. Rheumy blue eyes stared at Pia who smiled like a little princess. "I'm right here." She placed her small hands on either side of Mattie's hollow, wrinkled face.

"Love." The hint of a smile touched Mattie's thin lips.

"I love you too, Mama Mattie." Pia looked to her mother.

"See Mommy, it's magic," she whispered.

Norman held his wife's hand and gently brought it to his lips.

Her eyes moved slowly to Norman's face.

His expression pleaded with her to recognize him. "Good morning, Sweet Mattie."

He tenderly touched his lips to her forehead. Fearful of losing her moment of lucidity he continued talking. "Today I was thinking, Mattie, of the time we took Emily to the Enchanted Forest. I remember, Mattie, how you would kneel down beside Emily and recite each nursery rhyme to her and then she would repeat it."

"I LOVE the Enchanted Forest." Pia exclaimed excitedly jumping up and down on her knees at the foot of the bed. Sage reached out with a reminding touch for Pia to calm down.

"Emily's favorite was Cinderella's pumpkin coach." Norman looked at Mattie, "Wasn't it?"

The old woman smiled weakly.

"The pumpkin coach is my favorite too. I 'betend' I'm Cinderella." Pia giggled mischievously.

Sage sat quietly, watching and listening and remembering too when she and Eric brought their toddler daughter to the Enchanted Forest and had to bribe her with promises of an ice cream cone with rainbow sprinkles to get her to relinquish her seat in the pumpkin coach.

"You know," Norman looked at Sage then back to Mattie ignoring the tears brightening Sage's eyes, "It's magic. Eyes to eyes, touch to touch, heart to heart, soul to soul that brings two people together. But the memories are the glue that keeps two people together."

"I know," Sage whispered. "But he's gone. No more memories."

"There's time." Norman reassured. "You have plenty of time."

She stared at the old man, clearly convinced of his dementia. "He's dead, Norman. Eric is dead. No more memories."

"Ahhhhh." Norman shook his head and smiled.

"I'm speaking of you and Hawke."

Sage valiantly fought a two headed monster of fear and anger from her voice. "Hawke?" She swallowed her ire. "There is no magic. And the only memory we share is a nightmare. There is no glue in a nightmare." She loved Eric. Always did. Always will.

"I've seen the magic between you two, Sage. And," he lowered his voice as if others could hear this secret, "maybe I shouldn't be telling you this but Hawke mentioned to me, when I'd badger him about finding a wife, that he was looking for one-of-a kind and I quote 'Independent, fiercely loving, hardworking... someone like Sage Winters.'"

Sage was flattered. Shocked and flattered. "He never..."

"He's shy. A total recluse, bookworm. Nerd. And incredibly shy."

"He disguised himself."

"He certainly doesn't look like a nerd."

"No. Not anymore. He worked hard and long to find his real self. He's a really talented writer and a caring man. He just needed to work on his image."

"And Daddy scared him." Pia interrupted.

"What?" they both looked at the little girl who was busy watching a cardinal on the branch outside the window.

"He likes to scare people." Pia offered assuredly.

"Pia, that's not nice." Sage scolded. "Your Daddy would never..."

"He's only joking, Mommy." She giggled. "You know how Daddy likes jokes." When the bird flew away she pressed her nose against the glass to follow its flight.

Sage nodded, speechless yet again. Eric DID like to play jokes on everyone, so much so that at his funeral, while in the receiving line, she thought she saw him wink in her peripheral vision. She thought maybe this was another one of his jokes. Any minute he would sit up and be the life of the party. But he didn't.

He didn't.

And now Norman had her thinking about Hawke. About his eyes when she felt him staring and she'd look up quickly and he'd look away. Except for one time. One time in the kitchen when she felt the heat of his gaze on her and she glanced up and his brown eyes, boldly smoldering, stared into hers so that for an eternity she was mesmerized until Lowell walked in demanding a roll of duct tape to repair a pipe in the barn. And she thought of the way he tucked the wisp of hair back under her knit hat that afternoon before their walk to the pond.

And the kiss. The kiss that she had successfully forced from her mind came back now. She licked her lips remembering the hot, delicious kiss that made her head spin and knees tremble. The kiss that made her remember that she was not just a mother and an innkeeper, but a woman. A woman who had been alone too long. The kiss that made her momentarily forget Eric.

The kiss that made her forget to watch Pia go into the house.

Then, while Pia contentedly watched the cardinal hop along the tree branch and while Sage reflected on the magic of one kiss, and while Norman prayed for his wife to know him, in the silence where only the occasional beep of a monitor, a small voice whispered, "Love, Normie."

Mattie's whispered words brought a look of pure elation to the old man's features.

He grasped her hand with both of his and brought it tenderly to his lips, closed his eyes and inhaled deeply as if savoring the moment.

"Yes, I'm here." His tears fell to her pillow. "I love you too." His voice quivered with emotions.

Pia sat mesmerized at her post at the foot of the bed.

And Sage felt her heart break into a million tiny pieces as a love as old as time reunited with the quiet simplicity of a touching glance. Eric had looked at her that way in the past. Hawke looked at her that way, now. Infinitely precious, gently held, always loved.

Sage silently motioned for Pia to quietly come into her arms and together they left the room to let the two share some private moments.

Less than a half hour later a nurse found them in the small cafeteria. Pia continued eating her French fries while the nurse whispered to Peter and Sage.

Tears welled up in Sage's eyes and Peter excused himself and walked out with the nurse.

Mattie had passed on.

Chapter 17

It took a moment for him to realize that the cell phone in the front pocket of his jeans was vibrating. He felt a similar sensation in that area whenever he thought of Sage. He stopped running and sat on a snow bank at the shoulder of the freshly plowed road. The only people who had access to this number were given explicit request to call only in an emergency.

Since his mom was relaxing on a beach in Hawaii, and he spoke at length to his editor yesterday, it could only be Peter, the police chief of Silver Creek and a man he now considered a friend. He hadn't heard from anyone since Pia's return and more than once had to battle the insecurities of his former self. Peter would only call him if something happened to either Sage, Pia or Norman or if Sage had become serious with Lowell.

In that case Hawke knew he would delete her from his life. That would be impossible. It would be like snuffing out his own candle. She and Pia had become a piece of him. And dammit, he hadn't been able to write a word since that bastard, Lowell, handed Pia to Sage.

What had happened that morning anyway? Driving back from the nursing home with Pia, his mind replayed the picture of Sage's joy in having Pia back and the look of thanks and forgiveness Sage would send to him. And love. He wanted her to look at him with love in her eyes. It would be a soft look, shy almost, maybe afraid of the intenseness of it. And she would come to him and he would hold her.

Just hold her and let her feel safe. And then later, in the quiet of the night it would be just the two of them and he would show her exactly how much he loved her.

But she was a strong woman. Strong, independent and apparently, very unforgiving. God, he hadn't meant for the year long makeover to be interpreted as an attempt at deception. He had worked so hard to climb out of the suffocating protective barrier his mom wrapped him in.

And then Lowell intervened and took the credit for Pia's return, and, as Hawke watched Sage reunite with Pia, watched Sage thank Lowell and Lowell silently accept her accolades, he simply left.

Defeated.

Empty.

He saw that it was Peter on the display. "Hi Pete. Is everything okay?"

"Not exactly. Mattie, Norman's wife, died this morning. He's extremely distraught. Does he have any other family?" Peter's tired voice delivered the news with concern and compassion.

"Not that I know of." Hawke had visited Norman at his home on numerous occasions and hadn't been aware of other family members. No phone calls or photographs. "I'll be there in a couple of hours."

"Good. I'll be waiting."

When he finally arrived at the nursing home, an hour later than he had planned, he hurried into Mattie's room. It was an eerie quiet. The bed empty, stripped to the plastic mattress cover. The walls Norman had so painstakingly decorated with old photographs and one of Mattie's needlepoint pictures were bare.

Hawke did an immediate about face to Norman's room. Just last week he and Peter worked together to expedite Norman's placement in this nursing home so that he would not have to go through the red tape involved with a possible kidnapping.

Fortunately for Norman, Peter suggested that he be protected with a confinement contingency. The local court agreed and although Norman was disappointed he could not share a room with Mattie, he seemed relived to know that he would have others helping to care for him.

Then Hawke and Norman went through the old house, and Hawke helped Norman pack up some mementos and his porch rocker to make the transition less traumatic.

Hawke paused at the open doorway and once again wasn't prepared for the sight that greeted him. To his left Norman rocked slowly, eyes closed, sleeping in the comfort of his recliner, while Pia slept soundly on his lap.

Peter leaned against the dresser, arms folded across his chest as Sage ironed a pink, cotton flowered dress. A string of pearls, a pair of new pink slippers and a Bible rested on the neatly folded pink and yellow calico patchwork quilt at the foot of the bed.

"I'll take everything down to the nurses' station just after I finish this sleeve." Sage spoke softly

Peter noticed Hawke at the door.

Sage looked up from her task and turned to see Hawke watching. Suddenly the iron moved of its own volition and she burned her thumb. She pulled away quickly and brought her thumb to her mouth to cool the burn.

"You all right?" Hawke moved to her side in two steps and was pleased that she let him touch her to inspect it. It was already beginning to blister.

"Yes." Sage whispered as she withdrew her hand and looked at the bubble forming. "It's nothing really. I need to get this done. Excuse me." She turned back to her task and focused attentively on the ruffle at the wrist of the sleeve.

Having been subtly dismissed, Hawke turned to Peter. "Sorry I'm late. Traffic got held up."

Pete nodded. "Accident further up the road held things up."

"How's he doing? Hawke looked over at Norman, who seemed to have aged twenty years.

"As well as can be expected. Pia has brought him great comfort."

Sage unplugged the iron, gathered up the things at the end of the bed along with the dress and left the room without a word.

"I've got to get back. Danny called in sick. Says it's the flu. I've got to work his shift at midnight."

"Well for your sake, I hope its uneventful then."

"You never know." Pete cracked a wide yawn. "I'm already more than tired."

"I'll stay with Norman. Have arrangements been made?"

"Yep. Apparently everything has been done for thirty years. Obits been written, all paperwork done."

"Man." Hawke looked over at Norman.

He slept like the weight of the world had been lifted from his shoulders.

"No calling hours, but there will be a small funeral service on Tuesday morning. I'll be back then." Peter slipped his jacket from the back of the chair.

Sage came back into the room.

"Sage, I need to work tonight. We need to head back to Silver Creek."

Sage hesitated.

Hawke could almost hear her thoughts. Norman needed her. Pia was comforting the old man in ways Sage couldn't.

She looked at Hawke and he felt his breath catch.

He wanted to hold her, to protect her. He felt

her smoldering glance all the way to his toes. He looked down at himself, wondering if his black Henley and denim jeans, with worn white patches were a little too snug. But the way Sage looked at him, the slightly narrow-eyed glance of a woman assessing a man and finding him desirable...that look thrummed in his veins. *Stay with me.*

As if she read his mind, Sage only nodded.

She slowly slipped on her coat and picked up Pia's jacket.

Hawke gingerly lifted Pia from Norman's lap and wrapped her snuggly in a blanket.

Sage didn't say a word as Pia contentedly nestled against Hawke's chest and shoulder.

When Sage smoothed the little girl's hair from her face, Pia sighed and wriggled her face into the warmth of Hawke's neck.

"I'll carry her out to the car. Peter's warming it up." Hawke waited at the door as he watched Sage lean over and whisper to Norman.

The old man, still groggy, nodded, smiled and patted the back of Sage's hand.

She followed Hawke to the car, watched as Hawke placed Pia gently into the car seat and buckled her in. He closed the rear door. "Sage." He spoke her name with the warmth of a comforting hug.

Would he ask her to stay? Would she say yes?

She checked to see Peter waiting patiently behind the wheel. "I know we have to talk." She looked up at him, into the depth of his eyes, "but not here, not now. I can't think."

Guess not. But his heart leapt because she was speaking to him again.

"I agree."

She shivered as she inhaled crisp, clean air. "It's been a long difficult day."

He reached out and smoothed a tear away from

her rosy cheek. "We'll have plenty of time to talk later, when we both can think clearly."

She turned to lower herself into the car but his hand on her arm stopped her.

"In the meantime," he held her face firmly in her palms, "Think about this." He lowered his head, touched his lips to hers, traced with his tongue, tasted the hint of strawberry lip gloss and when she sighed he ended the kiss abruptly.

It was a challenge. A promise. A clear communication of what could be.

She slowly lowered herself into the car, fastened her seatbelt and watched him out her window until the car disappeared from view.

Hawke felt his spirits lift. There would be words. There would be anguish for Norman. There would be joy in Pia. And with that kiss, there were promises made.

The week following Mattie's funeral was hectic with Norman either so morose and unresponsive or so agitated and belligerent at being cooped up in the nursing home the nurses called Hawke to come down to visit with him.

He made the drive down to be with Norman almost daily. Consequently time would not allow him a visit to Thistle Dew, and, although he had had a few telephone conversations with Pia, Sage, who was either never home or too busy, never returned his calls.

****

Hawke watched the faint hint of sunrise lighten the wooded yard. His mind was not on the beauty of his surroundings but of the delicious flavor of Sage's kiss.

"Norman, let's go to Thistle Dew for a few days." It wasn't even seven am and the two had been waiting for the coffee to finish brewing. He set two plates of eggs and toast on the small table.

"I'd like that." The old man's smile wrinkled his eyes. "Bought a new book to read with Pia when we went to town yesterday, I'll go get it." Norman rose from his place at the breakfast nook with more enthusiasm that he had had for the past weeks.

"Norman, eat your breakfast first." Hawke poured two mugs of coffee. "Then we'll pack overnight bags. Oh, and bring your laptop. Maybe the muse has been hiding there." Neither of the authors had been too productive lately.

Hawke sat at the table and looked out the window in time to watch a moose stroll mightily across his yard. "It's time to start writing again." Hawke spread peanut butter on his toast.

Norman ate his meal quickly, set his plate in the sink and hurried to his room, only pausing to grab his pipe from the ashtray by the door and tuck it into his pocket.

Hawke smiled, inwardly pleased with Norman's improved healing. After two weeks of nurses' phone calls and daily trips to the nursing home, Hawke made arrangements for Norman to take up residence in Hawke's spare room. The elderly man had no one else, and Hawke appreciated many of the old man's attributes. He was a talented writer and offered his view on current issues with wisdom and humor.

Norman dropped his small leather bag by the door, then returned to the table. He took a gulp of his coffee. "Did you make reservations?" Norman paused, added another spoonful of sugar and sipped. "Will there be room? She's still pretty busy with spring skiers, you know."

"If there are no rooms left, I'll sleep on the couch and you can have Pia's room. She's volunteered to sleep with her mother."

Norman shot him a look across the table. "You've talked to Pia?"

Hawke nodded. "Last night." Hawke sopped up

egg yolk with his toast, took a bite and slowly chewed. He loved to tease Norman this way, making him wait for the end of a sentence or a thought. "Kristen dialed for her, but she called 'cause there was a 'mergency."

"Everything okay?" Norman grinned, knowing an emergency call from Pia could be anything from a doll losing an arm to a misplaced book.

"Seems Sage had a date with Lowell." Hawke chuckled. "Pia was pretty upset."

"Aren't you?" Norman looked shocked.

Hawke topped off his mug and gulped his coffee. "Damn! That was hot!"

"Are you?" Norman ignored Hawke's already familiar methods of changing topics. "Are you concerned that Sage had a date with Lowell last night?" Then Norman's expression changed as if a cartoon light bulb turned on over his head. "Of course you are. That's why we are going on this impromptu trip to Thistle Dew. That's great, Hawke. I was wondering when you would finally admit that you've—how do they say it now-a-days? - got the hots for her." Norman nearly giggled with delight at this revelation.

"Norman, please. I don't think that's polite. Not the appropriate terminology when referring to a lady like Sage. But, yes," Hawke smiled. "I do like her and I suppose I'm a bit jealous." Jealous. God. He wanted to drive out to Silver Creek and strangle the bum. Which was exactly what they would do. Drive to Thistle Dew. Sadly, the strangling Lowell part wasn't legal and Hawke didn't want spend the rest of his life in jail without Sage and Pia. Lowell would live. The bum.

Norman woke up from his mid-morning cat nap, stared out at the road they traveled and then interrupted Hawke's thinking. "You know, a gal like Sage is a rare find. Like my Mattie. Nearest thing to perfection, I'd say."

"She is, I agree. But there's a problem I'm not sure how to handle."

"What?" Norman stuck his cold pipe in his mouth. "That she is stubborn as a tree root? You need to consider that as a strength." He put his pipe back in his pocket.

"She's stubborn all right and definitely one of the most emotionally strong women I've ever met. And loyal. And therein lies the problem."

"You don't think she's actually attracted to that handyman do you?" Norman looked over at Hawke who adjusted the volume on the radio. "Cause if you do, you're dead wrong."

"No, I'm not really worried about him. But there is someone keeping her from wanting me."

"Not Pia. That precious little girl adores you."

"And I adore her." He pulled out to pass an eighteen wheeler that had been spraying his windshield with slush and salt. He maneuvered past the truck and pulled back into the driving lane. "No, it's not Pia."

"Then this is just another one of your excuses so you don't have to move forward here?"

Norman turned to look at Hawke. "This is the pattern of the former 'Hans Haakon Robertson.' Young Hans, so overprotected by his mother especially after his Dad died of a diabetic seizure. His step-dad turned out to be both verbally and physically abusive. And young Hans never had confidence in himself to make friends. Especially female friends."

"I'm not that scared young man anymore, Norman."

"I should think not!" Norman tapped his pipe and jammed it back in his mouth.

"She's still in love with her husband and..." Hawke hesitated. "You'll think I'm crazy."

"Who me?" Norman teased, raising his eyebrows.

"I think Eric is still taking care of her." He glanced at Norman to check his reaction.

"Isn't he dead?" Norman wrinkled his brow.

Hawke nodded. "And that's the problem. He's still in the house with her."

"You're not serious." Norman felt a chuckle bubble up in his throat. "A ghost?"

"No. More like a guardian angel. I feel it when I'm there. He's tried to get me to leave, but more important..." Hawke wondered if he should continue. "I'm convinced Eric's the one who led me to Pia."

"You sure about that?" Norman reached out and grabbed the door handle.

"I'm not so crazy that you have to leap from the car to get away from me." Hawke was irritable.

"You're talking about ghosts as if they're real. I'm the one who had the mini-stroke and lost my brains. But I'm here to tell you, I don't see or hear ghosts." Norman paused, frowning. "At least, I don't think I do."

"I know it sounds silly, Norman, but the more I think about it the more I am convinced." Hawke was sorry he had said anything now. It DID seem ridiculous.

"You know what, Hawke?" Norman concluded, "I think you're reaching way out to justify your cowardice at not telling Sage how you feel about her."

"What do you know about how I feel about Sage?" Hawke's coffee started to act up in his insides. He'd have to make a pit stop.

"Are you serious? It's written all over you, like you've got it tattooed on your forehead." Norman grinned as a rosy flush washed over Hawke's face.

Hawke flipped the directional and turned into a

rest area. "Need more coffee?" He stopped and stepped out of the car.

Norman fumbled getting his jacket on, then followed Hawke into the building.

"She knows." Norman added as Hawke hurried into the men's room.

Hawke swallowed hard to keep his breakfast down. She knew? How could she know? He never said the words. Oh sure he had thought them, had visualized the exact place and time he would tell her, but he had never said the words aloud. He had never even had the opportunity to take her to dinner.

Hell, they hadn't even shared a private moment together, save for that kiss by the barn- that one glorious earth shattering kiss that for all practical purposes had caused global warming. That one kiss sealed his fate. He knew then that he loved her. Just thinking about the kiss made his heart skip a beat. And hadn't she admitted the same?

Chapter 18

Kristen sat behind the desk flipping through a teen magazine when Hawke approached the front desk.

"Oh, hello, Hawke." She stood and opened the registration book. "Is Sage expecting you?"

"I didn't make reservations, no. Have you any available rooms? We need two rooms."

"I'm afraid we've only got Forget-me-not open. It has one single bed and a trundle. Although the McKays will be leaving tomorrow afternoon. That will leave Honeysuckle available. How long are you planning to stay?"

"We're not sure. I guess it depends."

From the desk in the reception area they heard Pia's screech at finding Papa Norman standing in the kitchen. "Norman and I came to get some writing done."

Kristen nodded, wrote up the appropriated paperwork, slid it across the desk for Hawke to sign and sighed heavily as if she were guilty of a devious plan.

"Where is Sage, by the way?" Hawke wondered why Kristen was troubled by his arrival.

"Sage?" Kristen repeated, using the age-old adolescent tactic to postpone the delivery of bad news. She avoided Hawke's eyes and scribbled something on the receipt.

Hawke nodded.

She wouldn't be untruthful. They'd bonded during the hunt for Pia and his search of the Inn's paperwork.

"I think she's..." Kristen's face pained considerably.

"Mr. HAWKE!" Suddenly a little whirlwind of pink and purple bounded across the room pulling a puffing Norman by the hand. "You came. I knew you would." Pia released her grip on Norman's index finger and took a flying leap into Hawke's outstretched arms. He squeezed Pia, inhaling the fragrance of strawberry shampoo from her tangle of curls and touched his lips to the little girl's crown.

"Uncle Lowell took Mommy to meet someone who wants to buy the alpacas. Mommy can't sell Pooh! I don't know what I would do. She says they're too much work now without Daddy and Uncle Lowell says he hates them." She sniffled and wiped the tears on the back of her hand and her nose on his shirt. "And I know why too." She smiled and couldn't control a giggle that bubbled up, "'Cause they don't like him. They do funny tricks to Uncle Lowell. Then they laugh at him."

Hawke loved this moment. He didn't exactly love that she used his shirt as a tissue but he did love the minty puffs of breath that flavored her story. He loved it when she wrapped her arms around his neck in a hug that nearly choked him. He loved that she looked at him with complete trust and... it was in this moment that he knew he was forever and irrevocable infatuated with, no.... in love with both Sage and her little spitfire of a daughter.

He knew he would do whatever it took to convince Sage that they, the three of them, were meant to be a family. As was his modus operendi, he was motivated by fear. Fear of the loss of two of the most precious people in his life. He would do whatever it took to make them his family—to make Sage his wife.

****

After an argument and silent lunch at a small

café they headed home. Little more than an hour later they both recognized the SUV that sat in Thistle Dew's parking are. Its silent presence only added fuel to the already volatile atmosphere in the red pickup truck.

"Didya' know he was coming?" If Lowell had been a snake each word would have dripped venom.

She moved her head side to side. *No. Yes.* She had hoped for it. Prayed for it. But never really knew if he was coming. "No," she said honestly. Her heart raced. Fear. Anticipation. Thrill.

"Well, I'll get rid of him. You're mine now. I'll make sure he understands that loud and clear." Lowell climbed out of the truck and slammed the door. He fast-footed to the porch, fists curled and ready.

Sage scrambled out of the truck and ran past Lowell to the door. "Lowell. No." She touched his arm but he ignored her plea and roughly nudged her aside. He pushed the door open with such force it banged against the wall causing a framed watercolor to fall to the floor and the glass to shatter. The room went silent.

Kristen, Norman, Hawke and Pia sat around the fire. Norman dropped the storybook he had been reading to Pia.

Hawke slowly stood.

"I want you outta here." Lowell pointed his shaking finger at Hawke as he huffed and puffed, his voice loud and slightly intimidating.

Pia ran to her mother, who until then stood paralyzed at the door. Sage held Pia in a protective hug.

Oblivious to the other people in the room she saw only Hawke. Their eyes met. Words crossed the room telepathically.

I'm here.
At last.

I'll keep you safe.
Forever?
Yes, forever.
Why?
I love you.
I...I... Sage looked away quickly.

"Come on, tough guy. Let's take this outside." Lowell taunted and rubbed his nose with his thumb like a ready boxer.

"I don't handle situations with my fists, Lowell. I think it would be an insult to Sage to have us assume that she would commit herself to either one of us, winner or loser, if we fight." Hawke stood his ground, fists clenched simply to reign in his temper.

He had been the target of bullying for too many years. But all that changed when three years ago as he researched martial arts to give his character authentic capabilities. He became hooked on the discipline. He still went to classes and although he had only a brown belt at this point, he knew he could seriously hurt Lowell with little effort.

"You don't think she's worth fighting for? Well, I do." With that Lowell reached back and swung a flying fist towards Hawke's face. The fact that his punch never made its mark confused Lowell. He scanned the appalled audience and reddened as the heat of humiliation crept into his face and broad grins crept over their collective, satisfied faces.

Hawke had simply stepped back and allowed Lowell's fist to trace an arc in the air.

It was just then that a large crow, perched on the porch railing outside the window, began cawing loudly as if laughing at a private joke.

"I promise you this, Lowell." Hawke squared his shoulders and then gambled his whole life on a hunch. "If Sage asks me to leave, then I will."

"Look," Lowell's adrenalin still clogged his thinking. "Sage has been my girl since we were kids.

And if Eric hadn't.. ."

Sage gasped.

"I mean...Eric was my best friend. He would want me to take care of Sage."

"Ask him." Pia piped up, intrigued by this dramatic display. "He's right here. He's always right here."

Pia's words silenced the room so completely one could have heard the metaphorical pin drop.

"Sweetheart, I don't think..." Sage kissed Pia's forehead.

"That's ridiculous!" Lowell turned to Pia, his face red with rage.

She snuggled deeper into her mother's comfort.

"Why do you encourage that, Sage? Do you think it's healthy for her to believe her dead father's ghost is still here to protect her? Are you crazy?"

Sage couldn't think. Couldn't breathe. She was aware of her surroundings and of the soap opera unfolding right here in her great room in front of the five people that mattered most to her. *Had her life come down to this? Had she lost so much of herself that she'd allowed Lowell to do her thinking for her?*

The two of them argued all afternoon because she had decided at the last minute NOT to sell the alpaca herd. She would handle the sale of maybe one or two as a business transaction but not deplete her whole herd. How had Lowell convinced her to meet with Anderson this morning?

The silence was broken by the steady rhythm of taps descending the stairs. All eyes silently followed the direction of the interruption as one lone golf ball bounced off each step until it reached the floor and rolled across the carpet to finally rest against Lowell's boots.

"See?" Pia taunted.

****

Lowell left the house too bedeviled to even

speak. What the hell was THAT??? Speechless, spooked and stupefied he stomped out to the barn hoping the group was intimidated by his apparent ire and not suspicious that it was downright fear that had moved his feet. He almost wet himself in front of everyone. He went past the stalls and out to the unused corral to relieve himself.

Fear grabbed hold of his throat as he saw the yellow word, written in cursive 'go'. He didn't need to read it twice to get the message. He didn't even give his truck a moment to rev before he pressed hard on the accelerator swerving into what was left of a snow bank as he sped out of the parking area.

****

The others gathered on the porch in silence, not able to put into words the events they had just witnessed.

Norman strolled out to the barn to investigate the final cause of Lowell's hasty departure.

"Come on Pia, I'll make us some hot chocolate." Kristen reached for Pia who still clung to her mother.

Hawke spoke softly to Sage.

"Will you walk with me to the pond?" She nodded shyly and reached for his hand. They stepped off the porch and started along the path that would lead them to a private spot.

"Me too! Me too!" Pia wriggled free from Kristen's hold and ran off the porch.

Sage sent Hawke an apologetic glance as the tall man lowered himself to one knee and chuckled as he caught the little girl in a flying leap and hoisted her up onto his broad shoulders. "'Let's go see if Lucky Duck and his family have come back."

Sage stepped back, hesitant and unable to move when her warring emotions suddenly settled themselves and a warm flood of love washed over her.

Hawke turned, watched Sage battle inner demons and reached out his hand.

She let him intertwine his fingers with hers and shuddered as he brought her fingers up and gently touched his lips to the united hold.

Together they walked along the wooded path to the pond. The snow had turned to slush and they were forced to hop over small puddles of mud. The trees proudly promised spring with their tiny hints of pale green buds. The pond, looked like a silver coin dropped in a lawn littered with patches of brown grass amongst the white. Ice chunks floated like cubes in a summer's glass of lemonade.

Pia squealed with glee when she noticed that the duck family had returned and proceeded to shimmy down from her post on Hawke's shoulders.

"Lucky Duck." Pia called to the male mallard with its glistening greenish blue head.

"Don't go too near the edge, Pia." Sage murmured.

Pia nodded as she ran, then glanced back to see that her spot met with her mother's approval. "Hi, Lucky. I'm glad you're home."

The ducks paddled through the freezing water to see if their friend brought a treat.

"I'm sorry I didn't bring you bread but I wasn't sure you'd be here." She apologized. "Mommy, we forgetted to bring bread for Lucky Duck."

"Tomorrow." Sage thought about the promises of that simple word. There had been days that she didn't look forward to tomorrow, days when she feared tomorrow, days when she hoped she'd die before tomorrow. And now, as she watched her daughter talk to the ducks on her pond in the near evening of an early spring day, while she watched Hawke stroll to the woodshed, she actually looked forward to the next day. "Tomorrow." she whispered.

Pia squatted down and continued an animated

conversation with the ducks, asking about their winter vacation, then replying to their imaginary responses.

Hawke fetched dry wood from the stack in the shed and after a little gentle coaxing and his old Boy Scout ingenuity, had a blaze going in no time.

Sage found an old red plaid woolen blanket and shook it free from dust, wood chips, unwelcome spider webs and dead flies before using it to cover a bare patch of ground.

Within minutes the three of them were staring into the flames, Pia contentedly snuggled in between the adults.

Hawke reveled in the sense of peace that enveloped him. The flames warmed his face and the company warmed his soul. He draped his arm around Sage's shoulders and pulled her closer, satisfied as Sage sighed softly. He tucked her under his arm and kissed Pia on the top of her head.

"Hey, you guys are smushing me." Pia squirmed out from the tiny space between them, stood just off the blanket and with hands on her hips she studied the pair. Suddenly her face lit up and she danced around in a circle singing, "You are my sunshine, my only sunshine, you make me happy when skies are gray..." She was circling around and around until she got dizzy and fell unceremoniously onto Hawke's lap.

As Sage leaned over to kiss her happy daughter, it allowed Hawke a moment to breathe in the perfume of her hair. His heart felt as if it would explode out of his chest as he contemplated voicing the words he had finally decided to say aloud.

A deeper chill crept over the three as the sun bid its evening farewell with a dramatic display of orange, pink and purple. Within minutes a sliver of a moon smiled at them. A glowing, flame-engulfed log popped, shooting up small sprays of sparks. Tiny golden embers swirled gracefully up into the darkness on wisps of gray smoke.

Pia watched intrigued as the flecks of glowing embers travel upward and seem to float right up to the sky.

"Where do the gold twinkles go, Mommy?" Pia held each of their hands as she stared up into the darkening sky.

To say they simply go out would be like extinguishing the magic of the moment, so Sage stroked Pia's hair and explained. "They go up to heaven. Watch them."

Pia studied the smoke and a few glowing sparks flying upward into the dark. "That's good 'cause Daddy can share our campfire with us then."

The three were content to watch the fire do their ballet in an orange circle, like dancers with iridescent blue tutus swirling as their graceful arms reach up into the sky.

Sage felt comfort in Hawke's casual embrace, comfort in the moment. *Could I feel like this forever? Yes, it would be so nice.* She tentatively rested her head on Hawke's shoulder. He adjusted a little to make her more comfortable. *Yes. This was a lovely safe haven, here tucked in beside Hawke.*

She closed her eyes and silently prayed.

Eric, thank you so much for the time we had together and for our darling daughter. I forgive you for leaving us. I will never forget you, but I'm ready to move forward. Please give me a sign that this is the right decision.

A little voice pierced the silence. "Twinkle Twinkle little star, how I wonder what you are."

Sage followed her gaze and joined her daughter's recitation, "Up above the would so high. Like a diamond in the sky."

Sage let Pia finish alone when she caught Hawke's expression and became momentarily lost in studying his face in the flickering firelight.

"I wish I may, I wish I might, have the wish I wish tonight." Pia closed her eyes, scrunched up her face and moved her lips as she silently told the stars her secret dream. After a moment of heavenly quiet Pia interrupted, "I have a really good wish."

Sage brushed a wisp of hair from Pia's eyes, "What is it?"

"It won't come true if I tell you." Pia looked mischievously from her mother to Hawke, "But you can guess." She held up three fingers. "'Three guesses."

Hawke guessed first, "I think that you wished we would go back to the house and have something to eat."

"No silly. That's gonna happen anyway."

"Did you wish for a new doll?" Sage guessed.

"No. Mommy. I have enough dolls already."

"I bet you wished for a big bowl of ice cream instead of chicken?" Hawke tried.

"NOPE!" Pia sat up excitedly. "Now it will be a secret forever." The little girl's yawn reminded them that it was getting late.

"I'll bet you'd like a nice warm bath about now." Sage reluctantly rose from her comfortable place on the blanket. "I hope there's still a little dinner left for us." She reached for Pia's hand and felt thankful once again for her safe return.

"My wish is gonna come true too, Mommy." Pia rubbed her eyes with her fist.

"Oh yeah? How do you know?" Sage watched as a deer scampered off into the woods.

"Daddy's star winked at me."

The girls waited at the edge of the wood while Hawke folded the blanket and returned it to the shed, then covered the fire with snow before he joined them in their walk to the Inn.

Pia reached up for Hawke to carry her and fell

asleep on his shoulder by the time they got to the place in the woods where they had once made snow angels.

"So what did you wish for?" Hawke held her hand, warming it in his.

"It's supposed to be a secret." Sage teased, a little shy about revealing her true dreams. "Did you make a wish?"

"Of course. It's the same wish I've made every night on every star, and in my prayers and on my birthday candles."

"And it hasn't come true yet?"

"Yes, I think it has." He stopped mid-stride in that shadowed place by the barn. The place of the first kiss.

"Sage, I've been wanting to tell you something for quite some time now," he spoke softly and her sudden stillness let him know that she was listening. "I hope I'm not alone here in thinking that over these past few months, as crazy as they've been, our hearts have come together."

He waited for her to respond but she said nothing. Fear started to creep up on him and he swallowed hard to keep it down. "I love you, Sage." There he'd said it.

She said nothing, didn't look at him, didn't react at all.

So he continued, "I have always loved you. I just had to wait my turn."

She stared at him; studied the evening stubble on his chin, watched him bite the inside of his bottom lip, then looked into his eyes. Love.

Her pause gave his other self moments to berate him. *FOOL! It yelled. You planned to tell her over a candlelit dinner with flowers and a ring. Just look at this romantic setting you chose...beside a barn, in the dark, holding her child, and all three of you smell like a musty old blanket and campfire. Fool!*

Tears threatened to sting his eyes. He turned away from Sage and took a step towards the house. Timing. That was everything. He knew that in his writing and in his martial arts, but when it came to this.. .this most important moment in his life, he forgot about timing.

She tugged at his hand to stop him. "I love you too." she whispered so softly he thought it might be the breeze in the trees.

He turned again to face her. Had he heard her correctly?

"I love you, Hawke." It was something, something at the campfire that must have opened her heart. "I love you so much." She touched her palm to his face, brought her fingers slowly down to his lips, as if remembering the promise of that first kiss.

He let the words sink in. Words that he had waited to hear forever. Felt the warmth of her palm on his face. So this is what it feels like to be loved. He wrapped his free arm around to hug her and when she looked up at him their lips touched. Love felt warm, heat and bright colors, like fireworks. The touch melted to a kiss, their lips fused until mouths opened and tongues sought more.

The outside world faded to black and only they existed. Only they mattered.

"This'll do." He whispered.

A tiny, sleepy voice doused the moment like a bucket full of icy water. Their bodies nearly hissing as steam seemed to surround them like a lover's aura. Pia lifted her heavy head, looked at each of them with a winning smile, "My wish came true." she wrapped an arm around each of their necks, three faces touching. "Did yours?"

****

Getting his message across to Lowell had not been approved by the elders but they had to contain their mirth as they gave Eric a mild reprimand. It was well worth the words to see Lowell run out of the barn and into his truck before he had thought to zip his fly.

"Ok sweet Sage. It's time for me to go. I can rest now that I know that my two most precious gifts will be loved and cared for."

Eric left with one loud POP! And spray of sparks from a log in their campfire and waved goodbye as he rode on a curl of smoke into the crisp heavens.

ALee Drake

Puppy Chow (Pia's favorite snack)

1/2 cup Peanut Butter
1/4 cup Butter
1 cup Chocolate Chips
1/2 tsp. Vanilla
9 cups Crispix cereal (any flavor)
1-1/2 cups Powdered Sugar
Instructions:

1. Combine peanut butter, butter and chocolate chips in a microwave safe bowl.

2. Microwave for one minute then stir to blend all ingredients thoroughly. Add 1/2 tsp. vanilla. Stir well.

3. Place the 9 cups of Crispix cereal in a very large bowl.

4. Pour the peanut butter-chocolate mixture over the cereal and toss evenly, making sure all the cereal gets a good covering.

5. Coat with powdered sugar, sprinkling evenly over the cereal and tossing as you sprinkle to cover each piece well.

A word about the author...

ALee (pronounced AY-Lee) wrote her first romance during the 2 a.m. feedings of baby #3. That first book, FLYING KITES, written in pencil in a spiral notebook, is tucked away for now but was the beginning of ALee's secret life.

It was a relief to finally release the characters and voices, their adventures and journeys to paper. Only when one story was finished, there were more voices, more characters begging for their story to be told. And so it goes...

ALee is fortunate to be married for 36 years to her best friend and travel buddy, Wlad. Together they have walked the volcano rim in Hawaii, salmon fished the Kenai River in Alaska, walked a section of the Great Wall in China, been to a Snake Farm (not her choice) in Thailand, strolled at midnight down the river walk in San Antonio (very romantic), and snorkled at the City of Refuge.

ALee and Wlad have five amazing children and three grandchildren.

Thank you for purchasing
this Wild Rose Press publication.
For other wonderful stories of romance,
please visit our on-line bookstore at
www.thewildrosepress.com

For questions or more information,
contact us at
info@thewildrosepress.com

The Wild Rose Press
www.TheWildRosePress.com

Other Faery Rose titles to enjoy:

THE SUMMONS by Jo Barrett
Was he real or had she lost her mind? Lindsay Sumner, an overworked nurse, isn't quite sure what to make of the handsome Highlander who is bound and determined to love her—all of her, body and soul.

THE DRAGON OF CROATIA by Valerie Everhart
Gavriel Dimitrios, the dragon of Croatia, is loose and with vengeance on his mind. Stubborn Callie Stewart, the woman responsible for his release from the ancient stone tablet, may be too cozy with the smugglers Gavriel has vowed to capture.

SOMEWHERE MY LOVE by Beth Trissel
Star-crossed lovers have a rare chance to reclaim the love cruelly denied them in the past, but can they grasp this brief window in time before it is too late?

COLOR OF DREAMS by Tia Dani
What happens when a Wiccan high-priestess and three mischievous nymphs conjure spells on an environmentalist and a jet engine designer? Could be magic, mayhem, and wild nights of passion.

KINGMAKER'S GOLD by M K Mancos
Gold—the word alone evokes dreams of riches beyond imagination. Whether one is a mortal woman or one of the fey men who inhabit New York in 1910, the precious metal can have great impact and far-reaching consequences.

ZORROC: FELINE PREDATORS OF GANZ, BOOK 1
by Lil Gibson
Legends, folklore, and science fiction all have a thread of truth as far as Catarina Achilles is concerned. One evening reality and fantasy merge to form a cat man she initially believes is a pooka. Before she can realize her blunder and divine his intentions, he steals her away to a world of deceit, betrayal...and fevered desire.

LaVergne, TN USA
23 October 2009

161774LV00004B/2/P